REDEEMING RIVER

Dan Smeenge

TM

All rights reserved

DEDICATION

This book is dedicated to
The Sunday Night Literary Club
who first heard it
in bits and pieces
during it's creation.

TABLE OF CONTENTS

Chapter One   Page 7
Chapter Two   Page 17
Chapter Three   Page 23
Chapter Four   Page 32
Chapter Five   Page 44
Chapter Six   Page 51
Chapter Seven   Page 61
Chapter Eight   Page 74
Chapter Nine   Page 85
Chapter Ten   Page 96
Chapter Eleven   Page 108
Chapter Twelve   Page 116
Chapter Thirteen   Page 124
Chapter Fourteen   Page 140
Chapter Fifteen   Page 153
Chapter Sixteen   Page 164
Chapter Seventeen   Page 178
Chapter Eighteen   Page 193
Chapter Nineteen   Page 206

CHAPTER ONE

If he had wanted to know, the screen would have told him how fast the plane was moving, how high they were flying and when they would be in New York, but his mind was on other things.

In his attaché case was his laptop and important papers. In the carry-on overhead was a change of clothes, camera, toiletries, a book he thought he could read on the plane (but hadn't yet) and a box of photographs. In the hold of the plane his luggage contained the usual assortment of clothes, books, souvenirs from his three years of living in Albania plus a bottle of *raki* that his neighbor had made. And somewhere in the hold was a six-foot long box in which was the body of his wife.

They said it was an accident. The police, the doctors, the bystanders, the driver of the truck that hit his wife, all said that it was an accident. There was one of those little three wheel vehicles, with a small but loud two cycle engine. It had a three-by-five foot bed in back that was piled eight feet high with four-by-six foot mattresses. The vehicle took the corner too fast. It tipped its load into the street. The oncoming car swerved to miss the pile. A truck swerved to miss the car.

Jack had stayed in the shop to talk to the man behind the desk. They had been in his shop several times before, and he had wanted to develop a friendship with him. His wife stepped out to pick up some coffee, the fresh roasted, fresh ground Turkish style that he had almost become addicted to. They would meet at the byrek shop on the corner. The oily pastry filled with salty white cheese was his favorite lunch and once a week she tolerated it just for him. The noise from the three wheel cart called his attention to the road. He had wanted one of those; he had even told his board of directors that they should buy him one. His wife thought they were cute too, and stopped to look at it.

Over and over, the events of that day played in Jack's mind, Their conversation of that morning about their upcoming trip home, the hope that water would be available so that they could do laundry and the need to "pop out for a bit" to pick up a few things. All so casual. All so trivial. They were out of coffee, he said. He needed some before tomorrow. They could get a byrek for lunch, he suggested with a smile. Over and over it played. If only one thing was different, if she hadn't gone to get the coffee, if he hadn't stopped to talk, if they had left a little earlier or later.....over and over, it was the same, the mattresses, the car, the truck.

Contrary to Jack's nature, he wanted to yell. Every time someone asked him something like, "Can I get you anything?" He wanted to shout "Yes, my wife back!" Or if they wished him a nice flight, he would be tempted to punch them in the face. They were not in his world. They could not understand the pain he was dealing with, he himself did not know it fully. He was still numb, three weeks after the accident. Three weeks of trying to find a doctor to sign a death certificate, three weeks of trying to find someone to do the embalming, three weeks of going round and round the city trying to get all the documents in order.

What hurt most was that Jack was not allowed time to grieve. There were letters to email, services to plan both in Albania and home, neighbors to host and a home to pack up. They had made no plans, everything had to be decided on the spot, all the details that Sue had been so good at. Now their mission agency has a policy, now they make missionaries have a plan for death on the field, but they didn't when Jack and Sue signed up, they didn't three weeks ago when they stepped out to ...

"Coffee?"

The voice made him jump.

"Sorry, I didn't know that you were sleeping."

In the split second that it took to answer the stewardess Jack saw it all again. The coffee shop, the street, the car, the truck, the impact. He wanted to yell again. Why was she bringing all this up? Did she know what pain it caused him to hear that word?

"No, no thanks," his brain forced him to say instead.

Jack had wanted to sleep but so far he was not able to. Every time that he closed his eyes he saw her.

They had met in college. Sue was charming, mysterious and smart. What more could a guy ask for? They were both economics majors with their eyes on making money. Their dates sometimes centered on the financial newspapers, checking stock prices, comparing their individual choices. It became their game. Whoever had the highest returns that week would get to pick the restaurant they went to for their Friday night "out". He would pick Wendy's, she would pick Chinese.

They were in the same class but Jack had worked for a year before college. He had chosen to do a construction job rather than work with his dad at the gas station.

"It would pay more," he told his dad.

His dad had looked forward to spending that time with him, trying to make up for the lost years taken by work. There had been a few weekends spent on the boat up north, on a quiet lake, but too few, not enough to pull the family back together. Jack, the only child grew up too independent.

That construction job did pay more, and with almost $30,000 Jack would try to pay for college himself. He was riding the waves of interest on international stock. His first year had profited him 29 percent, his second, 31 percent his third year was down to 20 percent but that was the year he met Sue.

That first semester together, it seemed like they had everything in common. The second semester Jack thought they had nothing in common. By the third semester, they knew that they were in love and were planning a wedding. What they did not know at that time was how God was working in their relationship as well.

One of their good friends was a Christian. Although she never was overbearing with her witness, her life was a testimony that both of them admired. After a philosophy class that she joined them for a cup of tea. She was mostly talking with Sue, but Jack was listening in as well.

"That's it," said their friend. "In a nutshell, Christ came to reconcile the world to God the only way possible"

"By paying the price that is impossible for me to

pay," added Sue.

"Yes"

"And then He sends me to Africa?" joked Sue.

Their friend laughed. "If you think that God would punish you for responding to His offer of love then you probably are not ready to accept Him."

"No I don't.... I mean, yes I do..." stammered Sue.

"Do what?"

"Accept Him," replied Sue

"We both do," added Jack.

Sue looked up and saw that Jack's eyes had also starting to tear up.

As the plane descended into JFK, Jack's mind reluctantly came back to the present. He glanced around, put his seat into the upright position then drifted back to the more comfortable past.

The first few years of their new Christian life were a time of great discovery. Experiencing the heavenly father's love healing his earthly father's wounds helped him not only forgive his dad but also provide the foundation for a new relationship with both his parents. Sue also found a new longing for salvation for the whole world in Christ. And as their love for God grew, their love for each other reached new depths.

After graduation, they had a wedding that celebrated not only their love but also God's love for them.

It wasn't many years after that when both felt that God was leading them into a new chapter in their life together. They felt it was one that would send them overseas. It was a decision that God affirmed time and time again as they went through the process of being accepted by a mission agency-- getting Bible school training and raising the funds that they would live on for what they had hoped would be years in Albania. Jack thought back to their first plane ride together. As the plane descended into Albania's capital airport Sue looked out the window. "At least it's not Africa," she said.

After Jack passed through customs in JFK, his flight to Chicago was uneventful. This was obviously a business flight. Most of the men around him were working on laptops or reading the Financial Times. They did not want to be bothered by flight attendants. Jack was blissfully ignored. He finally fell asleep for the first time during his long trip.

Upon arriving in Chicago he had more papers to fill

out. Then he had to meet with the funeral director. A hearse had been sent to pick up his wife's body. It was several hours after he landed that he finally collected his bags and went out into the rainy Chicago evening.

There was a young man standing there with his name on a card. Jack had never seen the man before. After identifying himself as his driver, the man picked up Jack's suitcases and headed for the car.

"So you got the short straw," said Jack.

"Excuse me?" replied his driver.

"Nothing" answered Jack, and let him do his job. Jack figured nobody else wanted to pick him up and he wouldn't blame them. He doubted very seriously that he would have wanted to pick up a recent widower missionary from the airport.

Jack was brought to the apartment set aside for missionaries. He could stay here, they said, until further arrangements could be made. Meaning, he thought, until he found a job.

The next week went by very quickly for Jack. A lot of people came by. Some he knew, some he was related to. Jack had no clue as to why some were there and Jack thought they probably didn't know either. It was just the thing to do. Go visit Jack. He remembered very little about the funeral and what he remembered he wished he could forget. It seemed as though he was on automatic pilot. What was hardest was what followed. The people were gone, the service was done and the pastor had fulfilled his responsibilities. He went back to an empty apartment.

"Now, what?" Jack asked himself.

He had never thought of what he would do next. Too much on his mind during the last.... how long was it? Weeks? Months? He wasn't quite sure anymore. He got up from the chair in front of the blank television and checked the calendar.

"How long can I stay here?" he mused. Logically he should go home, but he wasn't quite sure where that was.

They had sold their house and had given away or sold the rest of the furniture before they left. Jack's parents lived in a condo in Florida. There was no room for him there. He would not feel right about moving in with Sue's folks. He knew nobody in the town where he grew up. So where was home? He wandered around the apartment for the next few days occupying his time with making three meals a day, buying groceries and doing laundry. Home was here. But not for long; they made that clear. He didn't want home to be Chicago. Maybe that's it: he'd get a map and cross off all the places he didn't want to live in and throw a dart at the others.

What would he do? Somehow Jack didn't think that he could fit into the accounting world that he once knew so well. He suspected he was not ready for another mission position. Maybe he should just work at a gas station, or McDonald's.

Jack was surprised to hear himself chuckle. When was the last time he actually had laughed? But now, realizing that he had no place to go and nothing to do, brought a smile to his face. Why was that? Maybe it was just that all the other emotions were drained out and laughter was the only thing left. Maybe it was because it was the first time in a long time he had no responsibilities to anyone other than himself. Maybe It was because the responsibilities and duties of being a missionary were no longer his. It was this thought that gave him the freedom to dream.

CHAPTER TWO

If Sue was here she would've helped Jack sort out his thinking, but Sue was gone and it seemed that half of him was gone too. After what he had been through there was no job he could think of that would fit who he was now. And who exactly he was now without Sue he was not quite sure.

People told him to take his time to heal and figure out where he was going now in life. But where? The small mission apartment he was staying in would have to be turned over to somebody else by the end of the month. That gave him thirty days to sort out his life. He needed to go someplace, be by himself, live inexpensively, maybe on some deserted tropical island. Or build a raft, get a motor home, hitchhike across America. He fixed himself a cup of coffee as these ideas went racing through his head. And before he knew it he was finishing his last sip thinking why not? What was keeping him here or there or anywhere for that matter? A motor home just didn't appeal to him. But a boat?

Before Jack realized he'd made a decision the decision was made. Afterwards he felt the turbulence of the last few months smooth out like an airplane breaking through the clouds. It sounded silly, irrational, even selfish, but the more he thought about it, the more he thought it was the most logical choice he could make.

Jack liked sailing but wanted a big enough boat to stand up in. One with a good size kitchen or galley, he corrected himself. That would be about a 36-38 foot boat, with mast and sails to match. He would not be able to handle her single-handedly. What about a trawler? Too heavy on gas he decided.

How about a house boat? There were a lot of protected waterways in America. Jack decided his first trip would be down the rivers. He could start near Chicago and head down the river; down to someplace warm. There must be an empty Florida Key that he could stay on for while. The idea almost made him giddy. He checked his Rand McNally and saw that the river that ran close this bit of Chicago, where he was now, emptied into the Mississippi and ran all the way to Florida. He now had something to do.

Jack checked the want ads in the paper, but most boats were out of his price range. Those that he could afford were either too run down or had bad engines. He drove to a small marina only to be disappointed once more. Maybe paying cash was not realistic. Perhaps he had to get a loan from the bank, or work for a few more years before this dream became reality.

As Jack was leaving the marina he saw an old house boat up on blocks in the back corner lot. He walked over get a closer look. It was thirty-two feet long and the brand name was 'Seagoing'. That sounded hopeful to him. There was a ladder that let him get up to the deck. There was no sign saying it was for sale, but he nosed around a little bit. He checked out the engine. It was a Chrysler 315. He smiled knowing that he could work on this one. Climbing back down, he walked over to the office and asked about it.

"Is that for sale" he asked, pointing.

"Not sure," came the reply, "the owner is in the hospital or something. You could ask him. Let me check if I got an address."

He disappeared into the office. Jack walked back to the boat for a proper look. He checked out the hull, then went back on board. There was a bunk bed in the back of the cabin across from a bathroom. It looked small but usable. Then came a table across from a kitchen. "Opps, galley, not kitchen" he corrected himself.

This was followed by a few steps to the main cabin with the steering wheel, the controls, and a sofa. This looked like it could be made into a bed. Jack allowed himself to picture a morning where he would have coffee on the front deck somewhere warm with a palm tree nearby.

It was different from most boats that Jack had

looked at. First of all it was clean. Secondly it looked like somebody was in the process of fixing it up. Not that that was unusual. Most boats were in the process of repairs, but this one looked like.... well, that somebody wanted to live in here. The carpet had been pulled up. There was no sink in the kitchen, oops, galley, he corrected himself again, a few of the lights were replaced. A few others were missing. It did not smell musty.

He heard the sound of feet approaching on the gravel. "Here," said the manager, "the address says Baptist Manor. There's no phone number, but you could probably stop in there."

Jack remembered seeing the sign for Baptist Manor on the road at the edge of town. He looked at his watch. It was 3:30 in the afternoon. Probably no time today. Likely passed visiting hours. He headed back to the apartment.

Jack pulled into a shopping area on the way. "I need some milk, and maybe something for supper." He thought.

This was the logic in his mind, but there was a Marine Store at the far end of the mall. "I'll just pop in and price a few items."

Two hours later Jack left with a few magazines, a price list for lights, sinks, stoves, carpet, charts, pots, pans, and plates. It left him in shock. This concept didn't look feasible anymore. Everything cost far more than he thought possible. One could stay at the Holiday Inn for much less! It wasn't until he got back to the apartment that he realized he forgot the milk.

"Well, I'll just do without." he thought.

Jack was used to that. He was used to doing without the last few years for the sake of the gospel. But this was different. This is about a boat trip. It sounded selfish, but the more he thought about the trip, the more the dream grew within him. Gradually other options fell away. He stopped thinking what other people might think about it, too. It seem like the river was taking over.

In the meantime it was pulling Jack out of the pain and the depression he felt. It was like the river itself, the current, picking up speed, pulling him away from the bank, forcing him to become more and more distant from the pain and the life that he had lived. It got him moving, thinking and planning again. It seemed like the only thing that could. "God," he prayed, "if I do this, is this okay?" He felt a peace in his heart.

For supper he went for the last can of soup in the cupboard. He sat on the couch with the television on. Lately he could not stand silence. He was not watching it. He was absorbed in boat magazine articles on how to anchor, how to clean fiberglass and how to cook on a small gas stove. It was a culture shock to realize people were actually concerned about all this. There were articles comparing different types of refrigerators, GPS units and radios. All the prices were more than what he saw today.

"Maybe if I get a job for a few years and save my money." Jack mused. But then, on the next page he saw a picture of a boat pulled up to a dock at some sort of a park. It was on the Ohio River someplace. They were people of all ages having fun, playing, and eating, it hit his loneliness hard. He wanted to be there with them, now, not in a year two.

His mind drifted off to pictures of himself sometimes cruising with other boats, sometimes alone, fixing a meal on board while underway, going through locks, having time for reading, wearing a captain's hat. He needed a white captain's hat. He was in New Orleans. He was on an empty key in Florida. He was pulling past the Statue of Liberty.

It was three in the morning when Jack awoke, turned off the television and went to bed. When he got up in the morning he felt more sane. He determined to see if it this was possible, but he would count the cost and not jump in blindly. The first step was to see this man at Baptist Manor.

CHAPTER THREE

Hudson had started a book. He could probably write some more. But he could not recall where the thing was. Probably in the trash.

He stared out the window. His move to this place had been too quick, with no time to plan. One day he was at his wife's funeral, the next day, on his back in the hospital from a slip on the ice. They had been planning a trip. Fix up the boat, sell the house, put some stuff in storage and head down the river to Florida. He remembered calling their friends with the store in Matlacha. Even before he could ask, they offered a dock .

"Any time" they said. "You have a slip at the shop."

It hurt him to think of it. There was one thing after another. Nothing he could do about it.

They had a buyer for the house. One that would take possession in the spring, just when they were planning on leaving. Perfect. That would give them a month to work on the boat, a month to pack and a month to get used to boat life before they left. Then Minnie got sick. He had helped her through sicknesses before; tuberculosis, malaria, flues and colds. She was tough, and his years on the mission field gave him some knowledge of medicine, but this was different. She was tough, but cancer was tougher, and all he could do to help was to hold her hand through it all. It was all too quick. Within three weeks Minnie was gone. One week later the buyer called up. Something about the company moving him earlier, plans had to change, could they take possession in two weeks?

"Sure." he answered, without fully understanding what was going on. The next morning, on his way to secure a storage unit, he slipped.

He remembered the pain, he remembered the ride to the hospital and giving his nephew the keys to the house and car. He remembered the doctor saying something about a broken hip and surgery but then there were days he could not recall at all. Vague pictures of nurses and orderlies, closing his eyes in one room and opening them in another. People bending over him, some he knew, some he didn't. He even had a dim picture of Minnie coming and saying that everything would be all right.

They kidded him about finding a good way to avoid all the work, but in his heart he hated it. His nephew arranged the movers, found a storage unit, had the garage sale, cleaned the house and signed the papers for him while Hudson was flat on his back with his broken hip. At one point there were twenty people from his church's Sunday school class in his house packing up his things, deciding for him what would be sold, boxed or given away.

He had never felt more vulnerable, more exposed. He laid there imagining the volunteers from the church going through his underwear drawer. He probably knew who would be picked to clean the kitchen. They would eat the low fat, no sugar ice cream. They would have to. They would find the stash of gumdrops behind the bread in the second drawer. He was craving one now. He worried what they would think about those gumdrops more that what they would think about the beer under the sink. Every corner, every drawer, every box, everything down to pens and pencils that he owned. It all had to be been gone through, cleaned and packed by someone else. He wished that he were dead.

He wanted David. His son had flown home from India when Minnie was first diagnosed with cancer and was able to stay through the funeral but he was needed back in India. Hudson was proud of his son, on good days. Today he wished they had not raised him so well. Today he selfishly wanted David to not be the glorious leader of the work that they had started so many years ago. Today he wanted the ten-year-old boy that would bring him a cup of tea at four in the afternoon, every day. He wanted the teenager that would run errands for him on his bike. He wanted the young man who drove their jeep to the preaching points in the countryside. He remembered David going through the university, then becoming a partner in ministry and finally, a leader. He was proud of the progress that his son had made. He was in charge of a large team and oversaw a ministry to thousands. But right now he wanted David to get him a cup of tea, he wanted David to just take care of him.

His mind tried to pull up the verse of Scripture that said something about, "giving up lands and family for the sake of the kingdom", and he was proud that David had done that, but what about him? Didn't the verse go on to say that God would give back even more in this life as well as in the life to come? Would God give Hudson a son to replace David?

There was his nephew, but he had never been outside the United States. He could not share Hudson's hopes and desires. He was nothing like David. He only thought logically; never with any passion.

As he got stronger, they asked him more questions but still treated him as if his judgment could not be trusted. They brought him his slippers, not the ones he picked up in Turkey, on one of his trips, but the ones he got at the church Christmas party. They brought him his bathrobe, the new one that he hated, from his sister, not the old one that his wife had given him ten years ago.

What he hated most of all was when they said that they knew how he felt. Liars. After a lifetime of work and service, sitting was hell. When they came to visit they pretended not to see that. Perhaps they were afraid that he would drag them down into his depression too.

They wanted him to sell his boat. He couldn't bring himself to do that, for one reason or another. He wasn't quite sure why. Maybe he still had hopes of walking without his walker. Maybe he still had hopes of going to Florida. Maybe it was just the last thing that he and his wife had planned to do together and he wasn't quite ready to give it up. Maybe it was because when everything seemed so hopeless, he could be in Florida, on his boat, in his mind. David did not want him to sell the boat. David had looked forward to visiting them in Florida. Perhaps David was hoping he would go on the trip with his father; maybe someday when India didn't need him so much.

It was hard to be here. Most of the other residents thought it was a nice place, but everything around him got on his nerves. The color of the walls was a certain color of green that was found nowhere in nature. The light bulbs were all fluorescent. He hated the food. Having lived in India, with all of its colors, sights, sounds and tastes, this place was too bland, too dull. He knew it was hard on other people living here, but nobody knew how hard it was on him. What bothered him was the sameness of every day. How could anybody get better with all this boredom?

His thoughts were interrupted by a six-foot black man with a mop.

"Time to get out," Bill said, "I got to clean your room."

"Liar," said Hudson, "you just say that to get on my nerves. You don't have to clean my room every day. You just like to kick an old man around."

Bill laughed, "You may be right, but if I didn't come in here and mop the room every day, you'd never get out. You'd never move!"

Hudson started to wheel his chair out of the room.

"Not today," said Bill, "I've got to clean your chair too. You get yourself into your walker and use those little legs of yours."

"Good thing I'm a missionary, or I'd have some choice words for you," snapped Hudson.

"Good thing I'm a preacher, or I'd fire them right back," said Bill.

It seemed to be a game that they played. Bill making Hudson get up and move every now and then. The Baptist Manor did not have a physical therapist, just Bill, the janitor, who preached at a small Baptist church on Sunday. Even if he wasn't such a good janitor (the best they ever had, some say) the staff would never let him leave even if he wanted to. He seemed to have a way of cheering up people that were sad, comforting people that were down and getting under the skin of some people that needed a little prod to get going now and then.

Often Bil was heard singing old hymns in his deep bass voice, taking extra time to clean the hall outside of the room of somebody who needed to hear the old truths of the gospel put to melody. If he took time out of his cleaning job to sit with a resident and just listen to them, the staff never seemed to mind. So what if it was not in his job description? They would rewrite the job description to fit Bill. He also had a knack for remembering people's names and their children's names and their grandchildren and even some great-grandchildren. He would take notice whenever a new picture appeared on a desk. "That Billy is sure growing up," he'd say, or seeing a new baby picture, "Is this your Linda's new little boy?" And during his lunch hour he would eat in the cafeteria with the residents, moving to different tables every day, depending upon who needed a comforting word or just companionship.

Bill and Hudson sometimes discussed the Bible in

depth. Mission work, or sometimes even the second coming of Christ would come up. Bill would allow Hudson to be stubborn in his theology. But when it came time to move, he would not allow Hudson to win the argument. After all, how does an old man in a wheelchair argue with a six-foot man with a wet mop?

Hudson knew he had to be out for about an hour. So he hobbled in his walker down the hall to the common room. There was nobody he wanted to talk to. There never was. Maybe that's why he went there every day; to reinforce to him or to them the fact that there was nobody in this building he wanted to spend time with. After looking around the room for a minute, he would turn around and leave. On nice days he would go out to the porch and sit in the sun while Bill cleaned his room. On rainy days, he'd wander up and down the hall's bothering the staff with questions. The staff loved sunny days. Hudson knew not to return to his room until the yellow caution sign left the doorway. Bill made sure he waited at least an hour to take the sign down.

"Don't want you slipping on a wet floor," explained Bill.

"I was through here twenty minutes ago, and that floor was as dry as a bone," grumbled Hudson.

"Don't you try to tell me my job, or I'll just hand over

this mop and you can do all the cleaning here." threatened Bill.

"One of these days, I just might." Hudson would reply.

"Yeah, a young man like you should get out and get a job," Bill would say.

At seventy-one, Hudson was one of the youngest people at the manor. It was his hip that put him here, not his age, but some days. Hudson felt as old as some of the oldest residents there.

CHAPTER FOUR

Jack had never liked nursing homes. They all seemed to smell alike. Was there some government regulation that ordered a particular odor? Then there was the memory of visiting his grandfather after several strokes. There were numerous visits to the home, watching him get weaker and weaker, day by day. The smell brought back all those feelings: inhale hopelessness, breath in despair, exhale death.

He almost didn't go in. There must be other boats that didn't require nursing home visits.

"Oh well," he thought, "I might get a good deal if the old coot is on his last legs."

He didn't realize he was developing a picture of Mr. HT Rivers until he asked at the front desk for his room number.

"Oh you mean Hudson Taylor?" said the lady behind the desk.

"I guess. All I have is his initials," said Jack.

"Well, he's the only River we have here," said the receptionist, adding, "Although we do have a Miss Isippi, if you don't like the Hudson." trying to hold back a smile.

It took Jack a moment to catch the joke.

"Room 102, it's just down that hall, first door on the left."

It wasn't far down the hall, but it seemed much longer to Jack. The door was open and he stepped in. There was a man in a wheelchair with a mop of gray hair slumped down, apparently asleep.

"Excuse me," said Jack.

Without moving, the mop of hair answered, "Why? Do you need an excuse?"

When Jack did not answer, he continued. "If you do, I have a lot of them."

"Are you Hudson River?"

"Zzzzzz!" was the only reply.

"I'm sorry," said Jack, not knowing what else to say.

"Rivers," said the mop of gray hair, emphasizing the 'S'. "The Hudson River is a lot of water. Hudson Taylor Rivers is mostly hot air."

"Sorry," said Jack and paused as he looked around the room. "But I thought it was China." not realizing that his conversation was not keeping up with his thoughts. "I mean, Hudson Taylor went to China, but I see a lot of things from India here, Bangladesh, at least."

"I'm not 'the' Hudson Taylor just 'a' Hudson Taylor. My parents named me after him in hopes that I would serve as a missionary."

"Did it work?"

"Thirty-five years in India," said the mop of hair as he turned around.

"Wow!" It really wasn't the most appropriate thing to say, so he added. "We did three years in Albania."

"So, what do you want? Support money? You've come to the wrong guy. Praise? Try putting in a few more years. Three years? You're still green in my book."

"No we can't... I mean... my wife died there," Jack paused. What was there about this man, this grumpy old man, that made him suddenly feel that here was somebody who would listen. "That's why I'm here; the funeral was two weeks ago.... she died almost 2 months ago....."

The sentences started coming out choppy and short like bubbles coming to the surface of a pot of oatmeal. But, they came out, along with a few tears and all Hudson did was listen.

Hudson's eyes never left Jack's face. They looked neither surprised, nor condemning. They didn't even look sad. More than anything else, they looked understanding.

After Jack had stopped talking, Hudson was quiet. Jack thought that in saying nothing, it was the best thing anybody could have said to him. Then after a while, Hudson spoke, and shared part of his story. It wasn't that they were trying to compare who had suffered most, or had given the most or had cried the most; it was more of sharing hearts than comparing wounds.

About two hours later, Jack said goodbye and promised to look in again. He realized as he got into his car that they had never talked about the boat.

It wasn't until mid-afternoon the next day, that Jack had the chance to get back to Baptist Manor. It always surprised him how much time it took to do nothing. It seemed like now that he didn't have a regular job, cooking, cleaning and doing laundry filled the day.

The afternoon turned cool, reminding Jack that he had better make some decisions soon. Four weeks is not long when you have to sort out your life.

As Jack pulled into the nursing home, he surprised himself by actually looking forward to the visit. In his first two-hour visit with Hudson, he felt as if they had become good friends.

Hudson was sitting in his wheelchair again, with his back to the door. Jack wondered how many hours he spent staring out the window. He knocked lightly.

"Hudson?" he said softly, afraid that he would be asleep.

"Huh?" replied Hudson, as if he was waking up from a nap.

"Sorry I didn't know you were sleeping," said Jack.

"No, I was just off thinking," said Hudson, slowly turning his wheelchair to face Jack. "My mind wanders a lot these days. What brings you back?" He added, trying to change the subject.

"Well, I never got around to talking with you about what I came here yesterday to ask. It's about your boat," said Jack and watched as the slight smile faded from Hudson's face.

"Did my nephew send you?"

"No," replied Jack, "I was looking around for a boat and I saw yours. The guy at the marina didn't know if it was for sale, but he thought it was worth asking. It's really quite a nice boat and I think it would suit my needs."

"And just what are your needs?"

"Well, you see..." Jack hesitated, not knowing exactly how to express in words what he had only felt in his heart. He had never had to verbalize what his plans or dreams were for a boat. He felt certain in the direction he wanted to go, but not certain on how to express it with words. Here was the test. In a second he decided that if Hudson sold him the boat and didn't laugh at his at his idea, he would go through with it. But if Hudson thought it was silly, or didn't sell the boat, then Jack would find a job, any job and forget about the whole thing.

"Well, you see," began Jack again.

"Yes, I can see, and I can see well," said Hudson.

"... I'm not sure where to start. I need a place to live, and I'm not sure where I want to settle down, so I thought about a boat and with the boat I could go anywhere... that there's water." He added quickly. "And I figured living on a boat would be less expensive and give me time to figure out what's next with my life."

"Don't you want to go back to accounting or banking or something with money?" asked Hudson, "or do you hope to get back to the field?"

"That's just it, I don't know."

Hudson could sense the sincerity in Jack's reply.

"I feel the need to get moving in some direction, but not sure which direction that will take. I thought maybe a trip down the river would give me time or better yet, give my brain time to sort things out, no, that's not quite right, maybe I should say, give my spirit time." Jack paused, trying to figure out what he just said, not worrying that Hudson might not understand what he heard him say.

So Hudson spoke up. "I think you got it right that time. It's your spirit that needs time. When you're on the field it seems like you hear from God moment by moment, but here there are a lot of other distractions, and it's hard to hear from Him through all the noise."

Jack said nothing. So Hudson went on.

"I never put the boat up for sale, maybe because I always hoped I could still use it, You see, it was a dream of ours to do just what you're planning on doing. Neither Minnie nor I could stand the idea of a nursing home or an old folks home." Hudson wheeled over and picked up a picture of his wife. He lovingly stared at it for a moment then handed it to Jack. "We have friends along the river and some in Florida, and we thought we would rather face a hurricane in Florida on a boat than another winter in Chicago. But, here I am in a Chicago nursing home in a wheelchair."

Jack took his eyes off his own hurt and heart and looked at Hudson. He thought he had never seen a sadder man.

"So you don't think it's a silly idea?" asked Jack, placing the picture carefully back on the table. "The idea of just taking off and going on a trip. Not even for me? I mean, I'm not retired."

"No, no, not at all," replied Hudson, pulling himself away from the painful memory, "I think it's just the thing. You need some time, you need to get away, and I've often thought that a good river journey is better than a psychiatrist or a counselor any day."

"I never wanted to sell the boat," said Hudson, slowly. "But I'm not going to use it anytime soon." There was a pause. "They all want me to get rid of the thing, I don't think that they would trust me on it anymore, but I don't want to admit that yet," said Hudson, honestly. "So, for that reason, I'm not going to sell the boat."

Jack felt his heart drop, but only for a moment.

"No, not for that reason," added Hudson, quickly. "I will sell the boat to you however for the reason you need it now more than I do."

Jack was relieved, not only was he going to get a boat, but he had Hudson's approval of his plan. He wasn't crazy, at least, not to one old man in a nursing home, and right now, that's all he needed.

The rest of the afternoon they talked about the boat. Hudson asked for an amount less than the going rate for boats comparable to his. It was well within Jack's means, and he would have enough left over to fix up the boat and still have some for the trip.

"What are you doing for money these days?" asked Hudson.

"I have some personal income from some investments that will pay for food and maybe some gas," said Jack. "If I run out, I can always just wait or get a job balancing books for some marina or something."

"I didn't ask to be nosy. I just want to make sure you can do this," said Hudson.

They went on talking about what needed to be fixed

on the boat and what Hudson had already done. Jack assured him he could tune up the engine and take care of all the other repairs.

Hudson would have to contact his nephew, who probably knew where the paper work was for the boat. It would take him a few days. Jack gave him the phone number of his apartment.

"That's all right," said Jack. "Just give me a call and I'll bring the check over, or do you want cash?"

"I don't trust people around here with too much cash," joked Hudson, "I'll take the check."

As Jack stood up to leave Hudson added, "Don't wait for that though. You get started on the boat. If I heard you correctly, you don't have much time to get it fixed up. Just pop in now and then and let me know how it's going, okay?"

"Thank you, Hudson," said Jack as they shook hands. "I'll do just that."

Hudson looked happy, as Jack turned and walked out. Jack could not help but feel happy himself.

Hudson turned his wheelchair back to the window and watched as Jack got into his car and pulled away. Only then did the smile fade from his face. When Jack was there, and they were talking about the boat, he felt happy. Agreeing to sell the boat made Hudson feel happy. Now that Jack was gone, Hudson realized that he had only been happy for Jack. Deep inside he was sad for himself. He had been giving up a lot of things lately, and each separation from his former life hurt.

"Lord..." was all that Hudson could pray at the moment.

He didn't realize how long he had been sitting there staring out the window, feeling sad and sorry for himself. Lately, he could spend days doing that. His mind seemed to go round in circles trying to figure out what God was up to. He had amazing arguments with the Supreme Being. He caught himself at times, explaining to God what God should be doing. God didn't answer. At least it wasn't any answer to any question Hudson asked him. But God did answer.

"Trying to burn a hole through that window with your x-ray vision?" asked Bill, making Hudson jump a little.

"You keep surprising people like that. You could give us all heart attacks," said Hudson.

"Your face looks so sad, someone would think you're already dead," snapped Bill. "What's got you so down, and be quick, I'm on the way home."

Hudson told him about Jack and the boat and all that he was feeling. Bill had settled himself on the edge of the bed and listened patiently. When Hudson was done, Bill thought for a minute.

"Well," he said slowly, "I think you only have two choices, one, you can curl up and die. Or two..."

At this Bill got up and started to walk out of the room.

"Wait, what's number two?" asked Hudson.

"I'll let you figure that one out," said Bill, smiling as he left the room.

Hudson always thought of Bill as his best friend at the nursing home. But sometimes he just couldn't stand the man.

CHAPTER FIVE

As Jack pulled out of the nursing home parking lot, he felt committed to the course he was on. He made a list in his mind that he transferred to paper as soon as he got home. Things he needed for the kitchen, scratch that, galley. He had better start talking like a boat captain. He wanted two pots, stainless steel with lids, a cast-iron skillet, make that two, one small, one large. He would need a stove. Why wouldn't a camping stove work? He would do without a refrigerator. He would learn to cook just what he needed so that there would be no leftovers. He wanted plates, nothing plastic, but nothing too heavy. He wanted a decent coffee mug. He would make coffee in a French press. He wanted plastic bowls with lids, wooden spoons, potholders, tea towels. The list kept growing. He realized that most items could be found at secondhand stores.

Jack assumed the boat's beds had mattresses, but he would need sheets, blankets and pillows. What about sleeping bags; how cold would it get? What kind of clothes should he bring? He would be washing his clothes at laundromats, or maybe in a couple of buckets. Buckets, he would need buckets. What else would he need? He would have to wait to see what was on the boat. Hudson did not go into details, but he could look around now; now that they had agreed.

What did he agree to? Did he just buy a boat? It had seemed logical, but now it seemed stupid. He couldn't wait in the apartment any longer. If he sat and thought about what he was going to do, he might change his mind. So he got up and drove to the marina.

It was about 5:00 p.m. when Jack got there. The owner looked like he was anxious to leave. He walked over to where Jack had parked his car next to the boat. Jack explained that he agreed to purchase the boat and he just wanted to look it over one more time.

"Sure, I'll just leave the lock open on the gate," said the owner. "Be sure to shut up tight when you leave."

"Thanks," said Jack. "I shouldn't be too long, maybe an hour." With that he climbed the ladder and took a look at his new home.

Home? Could he really call this home? Jack had a small notebook with him and he started to write down things that he would need. He made another list of things that needed to be repaired.

"Start from the beginning, bottom to the top," Jack thought. He went to the helm turned on the batteries and noticed that there was charge in them. He checked the fuel. There were a few gallons. He went back and took the cover off the engine compartment and checked the oil,the conditions of the belts, the hoses, the wires.

"It could stand a tune up," he thought. He walked back to the helm. "Might as well," he thought, and he tried to start the engine. There was a groan and a cough but after a few turns the engine caught. It sounded rough so he turned it off.

Jack took a look around on the inside of the hull as far as he could. It looked quite sound. Then starting in the back of the boat he took a closer look at its condition. There were no leaks that he could see. The bunk bed in the back had two mattresses, and they both looked in decent shape. He would have to get somebody to explain to him how the toilet worked.

The galley was easier. Everything had to go. Not only was there no sink or stove, but the countertops were rotting. It looked like there had been a leak around the sink and the cheap particle board had just disintegrated.

"Well," he thought, "Home Depot here I come."

The rest of the boat needed little help. A nail here, a screw there; odds and ends that he would enjoy doing.

He found a toolbox in one of the bins. There was a saber saw and a few other tools. He grabbed the tape measure and started measuring for the cabinets. The ones overhead seemed okay. What struck him about the boat was that it was evident that Hudson and his wife had really cared about this boat. Most of the used boats he had seen looked abandoned and uncared for.

It was almost 7:00 p.m. as Jack chained up the gate and pulled away. On the way home, he passed a Goodwill store. He pulled in. An hour later, he pulled out with some used cabinets that, with a little adjustment, would do just fine. A double sink had been thrown in for free.

The next few days were busy. Jack got a check over to Hudson and talked to him about what he was doing to the boat. He spent a few days getting the cabinets right, putting in the sink, hooking up the plumbing and just enjoying the work he was doing. He found a two burner propane camping stove at a garage sale. He found a larger propane tank at the Salvation Army thrift store. At Home Depot he picked up some gas hose, and with a few clamps he connected the two together. He put the propane tank in the locker at the back of the boat and ran the hose under the floor to the galley. The next day he made his lunch in the boat. Now it seemed like home.

He bought a car stereo on sale and connected it to a separate car battery. This he connected to a solar panel that he found on sale.

"Now," he thought, "I can have music, even if I can't run the boat."

Several weeks passed. About every four or five days, Jack saw Hudson. There were questions he had and papers to get from him. He kept Hudson abreast of what he was doing to the boat. He noticed Hudson's expression and could not quite figure out if he was sad or jealous. He didn't want to bother him any more than necessary. He figured this was hard for Hudson to take. So he stopped visiting for a while.

There actually really was no need to see Hudson anymore, Jack realized. The boat was in his name. The engine was tuned up, the new numbers were on the bow and it was actually floating at its own dock. Tomorrow he would move onto the boat.

The marina did not have accommodations for living aboard but they decided to make an exception for Jack, seeing that he had to leave his apartment and he was planning to leave in a few weeks. The owner gave him a key to the office so that he could use the bathroom.

Two days later, Jack was sitting in an old plastic

chair on his front deck, drinking his morning coffee. He was crossing things off his list. He had taken the boat out on a few test runs. He felt at home, but there was something missing. He couldn't quite make out what it was. Something in his spirit pulled him. He couldn't leave yet. It wasn't that he didn't have his white captain's hat yet. He found an old baseball cap at Goodwill and ran it through the laundry. That would do just fine. He had the VHF radio, the flares, the anchors, all the necessary life jackets and other safety equipment. It wasn't that. He had his clothes sorted out. He'd gotten rid of most of them; what he had on the boat was easy to wash and fold. It wasn't that. He had blankets and towels and a washcloth. Yes, he even figured out how the toilet worked. The engine was running fine. He even found an old tape of Jimmy Buffett, so it wasn't that. He'd have to find out today. He had to, he was going to leave in a week or so.

The Marina owner came down his dock to the boat.

"Mr. Rivers called," the owner said. "He wants to see you, today, he said."

"I hope nothing is wrong," said Jack.

In the back of his mind Jack was concerned something was going to stop him; and come between him and the river. Did. Hudson want the boat back? He realized, looking back over the last few weeks, how important this trip was becoming. It was not only a new step, direction and opportunity, but he also realized how much he needed this for healing. It did seem selfish, even foolish. It did not seem like something a missionary should be doing. He wasn't saving souls. He wasn't reaching the lost. Some people might say he was running away. He didn't feel like that most of the time - just now and then, and this was one of those times.

He never liked going to nursing homes, and this visit would be the hardest one he had made yet.

CHAPTER SIX

Jack was almost shaking when he walked through the doors of the nursing home. Bill was doing some cleaning in the entry.

"Morning Bill," he called out, "How are you doing?" then, without waiting for a reply, "How's Hudson?"

"Best you go right in and find out yourself, and don't keep the man waiting," Bill said with a smile.

"Well, at least he's not dead," thought Jack. He had come to regard Hudson as a friend and to think of another loss in his life right now would be too much for him.

At first he thought the room was empty. In the corner sat the wheelchair. Along the wall was the empty walker and the bed was empty too. He was almost ready to walk out of the room when he noticed Hudson sitting in the easy chair in the corner.

"Jack, how are you?" said Hudson as he slowly rose from the chair.

His hair was combed. He was dressed in normal clothes. He did not look like the Hudson Jack had come to know. He looked somehow younger.

Jack tried to hide his surprise at Hudson's change. He went over and shook his hand and sat in the empty chair across from him.

"I'm so glad you could come today," said Hudson. "There are a few things I need to say to you, and it would be good if I could just get them out, all in one shot. I'll let you ask questions, but I feel that I need to get this off my chest."

Jack didn't know what to say. He didn't think that he needed to say anything. He was just afraid of what was coming.

"Well, let me drop the big one first: I want to come with you," said Hudson slowly. "I've thought a lot about it, and there are several reasons why I think this is a good idea for both of us. First of all you need somebody else on the boat to handle lines. Now, I'm not the strongest man around, but I could sit in a deck chair and hold on to a rope. If you're heading down the river like I think you are, there are several locks, and you need at least two on board to go through them. As you can see, I've been working at this." As if to give an example, Hudson rose and flexed his muscles. "I'm not quite all there yet," he said, laughing. "But day-by-day. I'm getting my strength back."

Jack still was quiet.

"Point two: I'm a good cook. I mean, how are you going to drive the boat and cook a lunch? Or are you going to tie up every time you need a snack? I can at least do a lunch, fix a sandwich or a cup of tea."

It surprised Jack that he had never thought of this.

"Also," continued Hudson, "who is going to take over steering the boat when you need to go to the bathroom?"

It surprised Jack even more that he had never thought of this.

"I have also traveled a lot. We traveled a lot, my wife and I, throughout this part of the United States, and we have a lot of friends in cities along the river. I've kept in touch with many of them, and it might be nice to stop every now and then and get a good meal and may be a chance to speak at a church or at least sleep in a real bed." Hudson paused looking straight at Jack perhaps seeing if his words were getting through. Then he went on.

"I don't expect you to give me a free ride. We, my wife and I, had been storing food for our trip for some time now. There is a storage unit with a lot of canned goods and dry goods, pots and pans and the like. We can go through it to see what you still need. I know there's a good first aid kit that we got together and I know a bit about medicine. I can bring that along if you need one."

Jack just nodded. He didn't want to verbally admit that he never thought about a first aid kit.

"And I have the money that you paid me for the boat. I can help with a tank of gas now and then. I don't want you to think that I would be a financial burden on this trip." Hudson was quiet for a minute, then he went on with a smile. "And what about those rainy days when you don't feel like traveling on the river? Who are you going to play cards with? I'm also good at Scrabble and checkers."

Jack watched as Hudson's smile slowly dissolved into a serious face.

"But I have to tell you the real reason why want to come," said Hudson softly. "If I stay here, I'll die. This is no life for a man who has lived more adventures on the mission field than most men dream of. This place is so dull. It was getting to me." Hudson lifted his face and looked straight at Jack, "I almost gave in to it and let myself be bored to death, but God and Bill gave me enough kick in the pants to get me out of that mindset."

Jack did not feel that Hudson was finished with his speech yet so he just sat quietly waiting for the next line.

"You've gone through a lot too. It would not do you good to be alone, Jack. I think that we could be good for each other; to work through some healing. I think we can understand each other ... we have both been there."

Jack understood that he had just been paid a compliment. Hudson felt that Jack was a peer, a fellow missionary.

"I think if I listen to my own speech I would be unclear as to whether I want you to realize that I am a valuable asset to your trip or whether I want you to take pity on an old man." Hudson let his words sink in, "Either way, I don't care. I really want to come. I think it would be best for both of us, but it's your boat, it's your trip, it's your decision." Hudson waited, then added, "So what do you think?"

Jack did not have to think very long. He really didn't think he had any choice. Not that he felt pressured, it was more of a relief.

"Well I have a few points myself," Jack started. "First of all, I drink coffee not tea. You will have to learn to make a cup of coffee, Turkish style would be best. Second I like backgammon and prefer it to checkers. Other than that, I only have one question."

"And that would be ...?" waited Hudson.

"When do you want to move on board?" asked Jack.

"Good," Hudson said with a smile. "how about this weekend?"

"Okay," replied Jack with a smile. He now knew what was missing, and he knew that he had found it.

"If you have time today, we could go by the storage unit and I can show you what I have," said Hudson.

"Sure," said Jack. "I have the use of a car for about four more days. If you're ready, let's go."

Hudson grabbed two canes and slowly made his way out to Jack's car. Jack was not sure how much to help or how much to encourage independence. He assumed correctly that Hudson was the kind of man that would ask if he needed help.

The rest of that day was spent going through boxes and sorting out things that they might need. Some things Jack already had, but he realized that Hudson had thought more about living on a boat than he ever did. He chose to keep Hudson's stainless steel bowls and bring his plastic ones back to the thrift store. He gladly accepted the first aid kit and several wool blankets. There was also a box of books that Hudson insisted on bringing, one of them being an old Methodist hymnal.

Gradually Jack grew alarmed at the amount of things piling up in his trunk. Where was he going to find room for all this in the boat? Some of it he did not see any reason for. Flowerpots, for instance. Did Hudson want to grow daisies on the deck? Most of the food they brought, but Jack was a little hesitant about some of the boxes that only had Indian writing on them.

"Lunches might get interesting." he thought.

They had to tie the trunk shut with one of Hudson's old belts to fit it all in.

They stopped at Subway for lunch, Hudson's treat. He insisted. As they sat there, Jack looked at the people who glanced at them. Did they think they were father and son and that he was bringing his dad to a nursing home? Reality was funnier. Here he was helping him escape from a nursing home. He thought about what each of them had gone through. Most of these people would not have the ability to understand. Not for the first or last time, Jack was very glad he had met Hudson and was now going down the river with him.

When they got to the boat, Hudson stopped and just looked at it sitting at its dock. He had a satisfied smile on his face.

"I see you kept the name," said Hudson as he made his way down the dock.

"Yes, it seemed to fit."

With Hudson needing two hands for his canes, Jack was left to do all the carrying. But as soon as he got back to the boat with another load, the first one had mysteriously disappeared into the nooks and crannies of the boat.

Hudson would take the bottom bunk in the back of the boat as it was closer to the toilet and was on the same level as the galley. Jack would sleep on the hide-a-bed in the front part.

Somehow all the food got put away; the flower pots secured on the back deck; Hudson's clothes in a duffel bag on the top bunk and his books along the shelf next to the table. One book, Hudson pulled back off the shelf.

"Do you have a log" he asked

"What do you mean?" Jack asked.

"A log book, you know, where you mark down every day how far you've gone and notes about the trip."

"Oh, not yet."

"Well, here, we can use this one. Seeing that you didn't change the name of the boat it still works," said Hudson as he handed over a large notebook whose hard cover was decorated with Indian sari cloth.

Jack took the book. Admiring the cover, he opened it to the first page and read, "The record of the voyage of the ship 'EKBALO'"

"I often wondered why you picked the name," said Jack.

"At first, I told people it meant 'sent' as in one sent to the harvest field," Hudson replied.

"I know," said Jack, "but it also means 'kicked out' or 'cast out' as in Jesus casting out demons or the dog returning to what it "ekbalo'ed'"

"I see you know your Greek," said Hudson. "Some days I translate it differently myself."

With things put away they sat at the table, drinking some water.

"Promise me something," said Hudson after a period of quiet. "If I ever get on your nerves let me know."

"Only if you will do the same," replied Jack.

"Agreed," said Hudson. "Now you better get me back to the home. If I'm gone too long they will send out a search party."

"What are they going to do when you move out?"

"Well most of the residents will probably think that I died, and I hate to admit that the way that I behaved at first, most of the staff would just be glad I'm gone," he replied sadly.

Back at the home, Hudson explained to the staff he was moving out on Sunday. They questioned him at length about where he was going to stay and who was going to take care of him. When Hudson introduced Jack and explained about the boat, at first were going to refuse to let him go. But both Hudson and Jack convinced them it was going to work. In the end there was a form that Jack had to sign, accepting responsibility for Hudson's well-being.

Back at the boat later that night Jack made supper. It took him longer than usual, for things had been moved around. It would take him a little time to readjust from it being 'his' boat to 'their' boat. It felt different, but more complete.

CHAPTER SEVEN

Saturday morning, Bill had helped Hudson move the rest of his things into the now over crowded storage shed.

"There they can sit," he told Bill, "'til Jesus comes."

True to scripture, Bill replied, "Come soon, Lord Jesus."

"Amen, but just in case, I paid a year in advance so I don't have to worry."

They stopped off at Bill's house on the way back to the home. His wife had greeted him like family though this was the first time they had met.

"Hudson," Bill said, introducing him to his wife as he helped him get out of his pickup and unfold the walker. She wiped dish soap off her hands and gave him almost too big a hug.

"Bill has told us so much about you," she said with a smile."Come in and sit a spell."

Over pieces of apple pie and coffee they discussed his upcoming trip. "Yes, we will live on the boat, no, I don't know much about Jack, but he seems a nice enough fellow."

Questions about food, maps, storms, even how the toilet worked, seemed to make Hudson nervous about the trip. Out of self preservation, he changed the subject to their kids. Even though he had known Bill for about a year and had many conversations with him, he had not known much about his family. Almost as if on cue, in walked his oldest son from the garden. His clothes showed evidence of hard work, but his face and hands were clean and fresh from the spigot outside.

"B.J., this is Mister Hudson, Hudson, my son Bill Jr."

B.J. shook his hand and greeted him politely. Although he was only about twelve or thirteen, he behaved with more maturity than most college kids. He and his dad had a brief conversation about the vegetables in the garden, the need for rain and the worms he found for fishing. He then cut himself a piece of pie, poured a glass of milk and sitting across from Hudson started in on his own list of questions. It was clear that his dad did not just sit in front of the TV when he got home, but shared his day with his family.

After the pie and the milk were finished, the napkin carefully folded and placed on the table, B.J. excused himself to go fishing. He disappeared into what was probably his room and reappeared with a book under his arm. He grabbed the fishing pole almost as an afterthought as he went out the back door.

"Nice kid," remarked Hudson. "You can tell he knows he is loved."

"God first, then my wife, the kids come third. That's the order and they know it."

"Kids?" asked Hudson, emphasizing the plural.

"The two youngest are over at some friend's house. Sorry you missed them. Two girls, Mary and Elizabeth. They'll be sorry too. They asked me last night if it was alright if they prayed for you too when they say their good night prayers."

"Thank them for me, I have never given up the need for prayers."

"Ha," Bill laughed, "not on this side of the river."

It took a second for Hudson to figure out Bill wasn't talking of the Illinois River.

"Better get you back, can't have you missing lunch." said Bill.

Lunch. The word brought up smells from the cafeteria. Sitting in this little house, with all it's aromas of home and food cooked with love, Hudson realized what a sacrifice Bill was making to sit and eat his lunch at the home with the residents.

Sunday finally arrived. The early morning threat of rain had disappeared by the time most of the residents were up. By then Hudson had his clothes in two small duffels and the rest of his belongings in a plastic tub with a lid.

After breakfast Hudson sat in the dining hall till the service. It went as predicted, three hymns sung slow and off key, a sermon on the love of God, comfort and peace and a closing hymn that some of the residents didn't stay around to hear.

This Sunday was different. Hudson stayed behind to talk to the pastor.

"Pastor Smith, my name is Hudson, I'll make this quick, I've been a missionary and I've learned a few things that you could benefit from. Now I don't have the time to sit and teach you everything, nor would you necessarily treasure time spent with an old man, but I've picked out some books and I'm giving them to you in hopes that you will read them. If you choose not to, give them to someone else, OK? Don't let them sit on a shelf. Do you agree?"

He hardly gave the man a chance to respond or even think about what he said. He handed the bag to the man and wheeled back to his empty room.

Lunch was tasteless meat on boiled-to-mush noodles, green beans canned before the war, and a lifeless salad. With desert, they played the normal game of 'what's this'. Hudson guessed cobbler but the man across from him won by saying peach cobbler.

At 1:00 p.m. Jack pulled up out front and helped him load the walker in the trunk and the duffels and box in the backseat next to a young man Hudson had not seen before.

"Oh," said Jack, remembering his manners. "This is Mike. He and his wife are staying at the apartment. They are going out to South America in a few months."

"Where about are you going?" asked Hudson.

"Brazil. We hope to do some church planting or maybe teach at the Bible school," came the reply.

"Brazil? I don't think they need you as much as some of the Middle Eastern countries." Then turning to Jack, Hudson continued the conversation almost as if Mike was not there.

"Why do people send workers to places where there are plenty of workers already? Why don't they look at where the work is needed? What army would send more cooks and accountants to the

Pentagon when what was needed was soldiers on the frontline?"

Jack let these questions go unanswered, and Mike didn't seem to have anything else to add.

"I suppose," continued Hudson after a pause, "you go where you're sent. Maybe God has a plan for people to bunch up in places that have already been reached. It just doesn't make sense to me. But then again God never put me in charge. Good thing too."

Mike seemed relieved when they got to the marina and he could help unload and head back to his own world.

Jack and Hudson slowly went down the dock and fit the last few things onto the boat. As it was about three in the afternoon, Hudson suggested they have a cup of tea so Jack heated up some water. While they were waiting Jack showed Hudson how the stove functioned, and how the sink worked with its two faucets.

"This one will work when we have a hose hooked up to a faucet at a marina. And I put in a small hot water heater so that we could have hot showers and hot water for dishes. This other faucet works with this foot pump from the tank in the hold. We'll use this when we are under way. If we need hot water we will have to heat it on the stove while we're on the river."

When the water came to a boil on the stove, Hudson got out some tea and Jack got out his coffee press. They rummaged through the cupboards until they found something to go with their drinks. Jack was going to go to the front where he usually had his coffee, but thinking that Hudson might not make it up the stairs easily, he sat down at the table. He could already see there were going to be some adjustments that would need to be made.

After their coffee and tea was done, Jack had Hudson walked around the boat inside and out to see how Hudson could make out. It took him a little bit of effort to get up the stairs but as it had two railings he could do it. While they were up there in the forward part Jack started to show Hudson the controls of the boat when he suddenly realized that this was Hudson's boat and he would know. He stopped mid-sentence and realized the awkwardness of the situation. Was this Hudson's boat? Was this his? Hudson felt the awkwardness too and turned to go out on to the front deck. He noticed that Jack had gotten a second chair for him.

"Look Jack, I know this is awkward," said Hudson, answering the question on Jack's face, "but I think we can work out living on this boat together. I don't want you to go through too much to make sure that I can do anything. I worked hard trying to get my strength back and as time goes by I'll be able to do much more. Don't try to pamper me. And I do realize this is your boat, what you want to do or don't want to do on it or to it is fine with me. We don't have to go to Florida. We could stop anywhere you want to. You are not committed to get me anywhere. This trip is my risk. If I can't make it or if we can't get along, you can put me off at the nearest city and I'll make my way back here by bus or find a place somewhere along the way."

Jack really didn't know what to say. He didn't want Hudson to feel that way. He wanted to reassure him that this trip would be all right; that he could adjust to having Hudson on board, but he didn't know how to make that clear.

"And then of course," Hudson added with a big grin, "should I die on you, you can just bury me at sea or lake or river or wherever we are."

"Same here," laughed Jack. "Let's hope it doesn't come to that. I'd have a hard time explaining to your next of kin."

Jack decided a couple more handholds would be handy. As they didn't have access to a vehicle anymore, Jack rummaged through what the Marina had on hand as far as things to use for handholds.

What he found was some grey pipe and elbows that he fastened to the walls. He put one across from the bathroom and one in the bathroom itself.

By the time he was finished Hudson had already started making supper. He started with a can of mixed vegetables and added a heap of spices, not measuring anything. He had a pot of rice cooking on one burner and his vegetable mix in a cast-iron skillet on the other. Jack got concerned with the various things that he was throwing in the pan, but the aroma that filled the boat made his mouth water.

When Jack was finished his work, and had cleaned up in the bathroom at the Marina, supper was ready.

It was Jack's first Indian meal. He loved it. His taste buds were experiencing things they had never tasted before. To Hudson it was like coming home again. Hudson's face was that of a man taking a breath of air after being underwater for too long or taking a drink of water after being in the desert for days. Jack could almost see color returning to Hudson's face.

"Ah." was all Hudson said during the meal.

"This is going to work," thought Jack.

That evening they unpacked the rest of Hudson's things. They perused some of his books and soon Hudson's head was drooping.

"Well, I guess the night nurse is not going to tuck me in," Hudson said when his head jerked up for the second time. "I hope you don't snore," he added as he headed to bed. But it was Hudson that added music to the otherwise quiet night.

The next morning it was as if the boat had been home to the both of them for a long time. Their routines blended as each one went about their own business. Jack was fixing something on the boat so Hudson did up the breakfast dishes. Then Hudson went on deck with his Bible and hymnal. This was to be his routine every day: read, pray then sing a hymn quietly to himself. After some small talk, Hudson became deeply involved with a book so Jack made lunch. When he looked around to call Hudson to the table he was nowhere to be found. Stepping out onto the dock, he saw Hudson talking with the owner of the Marina. When he got closer he was able to overhear Hudson quoting Proverbs 30:18 and 19.

"Solomon said there are some things that were just amazing." Hudson was explaining, "An eagle in the sky, snake on a rock and a ship on the sea. He also mentioned in the same list the relationship between a man and woman, so you suppose he's thinking that there is a spiritual relationship between the boat and water?"

Jack did not wait for the man's reply but decided to hold lunch until Hudson was done.

Hudson was back in the boat in a few minutes.

"How did your talk go? I never thought he was into spiritual things." asked Jack.

"All people are spiritual and are always into spiritual things, they just don't realize it. And all talk is spiritual too, if you think about it. I think maybe I planted a seed to get him thinking more about God." Hudson replied. "You see, most people think evangelism is trying to get somebody to say a prayer."

"You don't?"

"No, to me it's more of finding out where a person is spiritually and getting them to take the next step. That may include prayer but remember that's only one point in a very long spiritual journey, and not the end, like some people think."

Jack found himself pondering this throughout lunch.

By the end of the day they realized they had to make a joint decision.

"So when are we going to go anywhere?" asked Hudson.

"Never picked a date yet, I thought it would take us a while to get the boat sorted out, now that there's two of us. Maybe by the end of the week? What do you think?" replied Jack.

"Well, let me give you some advice an old missionary gave me once," said Hudson. "If you never go, you never get there."

"We'll need to stock up on some supplies first, and we don't have a car anymore," said Jack, thinking out loud.

"See if the owner of the Marina will take you into town tomorrow. He's got a pickup truck that should hold enough groceries for a week," Hudson said laughing.

The rest of that evening they made out menus and listed provisions that they would need. Jack was glad Hudson was there, for it was Hudson that remembered the toilet paper.

The next morning the owner did take Jack and drop him off at the store while he ran other errands. By noon they had the food stored away and a full tank of gas. Two more five gallon cans of gas were secured on the back deck. Several one gallon plastic jugs of clean drinking water were put under the seat in the galley. And while Hudson cleaned the dishes from lunch, Jack, without any fanfare, started the engine and undid the lines. By the time the dishes were done, they were out of the marina and on the way down the river. Hudson made his way to the forward cabin with a fresh cup of tea and sat down on the couch turning his head to look out the front of the boat.

"This is better," he said softly.

"I could not agree more," said Jack.

CHAPTER EIGHT

Ship's Log:
Day 1
September 5, Tuesday.
"We made about thirty-five miles today in just under five hours. The engine is running fine which was my biggest concern. We are tied up to the city dock of some town that I don't know the name of. Went into town to grab a bite to eat instead of cooking anything ourselves. Not that I would've minded Hudson making another supper. I really enjoy his Indian style cooking, but we just had a hankering for hamburgers.

I was worried about what Hudson would do all day while I was steering the boat. I don't think I'll have to worry about that. There is always something that needs cleaning or putting away. (Boats seem to get dirty fast and clutter accumulates quickly on board.) At 3:30 he appeared with a cup of coffee for me and a cup of tea for himself and the rest of the cookies that we had opened up yesterday. This afternoon tea time seems to be a habit of his that I'm going to enjoy getting used to.

The current here is not that strong and the river is pretty calm. Our charts are old, but I have not found any discrepancies in them yet. Steering the boat is not as boring as I had thought it would be. You have to keep an eye out for the buoys and follow them on the chart. Then there are a few floating objects you don't want to hit. Saw tree branches and at least one old Styrofoam cooler today.

I'm surprised I've written so much already. I thought a ship's log was just about distance and weather. I suppose in addition to the journey that the boat is taking this book might help me record the journey I'm personally taking. Already today I have found a bit of peace from being on the river. It surprised me. I did not expect it. I thought I would be nervous and apprehensive about doing a trip like this. It's like when you read the charts you know there's a curve in the river, but the beauty of the river bank surprises you when you get there. Around each new bend is something that you've never seen before and no chart can prepare you for that. So maybe by the end of this trip I'll be surprised as to where I personally end up. Where that will be I don't know, but just like I need to follow the river and go where it leads me, I'll let God determine where I end up.

Hudson is on the forward deck just watching birds. I challenged him to a game of backgammon, but he said he was too busy.

The day was warm but the evening is cooling off quickly. Without a heater we will need our wool blankets tonight.

I put the eggs, cheese and milk in a box on the back deck. That should keep them cool enough through the night. We don't have a refrigerator or an ice chest so when the milk gets sour we will have to use instant until we get to a town again.

The crickets have started singing. I just hope that they are loud enough to drown out Hudson's snoring.

Ship's Log:
Day 2
September 6, Wednesday.
I do not snore, Jack on the other hand mumbles in his sleep. I found this out when I got up to use the bathroom in the middle of the night and found him in a conversation with the bullfrogs. It has taken me a few nights to get used to where the bathroom is on this boat. Jack says we should use "head" instead of bathroom, and "galley" instead of kitchen but I'm just too old to learn a new language at this point in time. Besides it's a home as well as a boat.

We went through our first lock today and we survived. My position is at the back of the boat with a plastic chair, a long pole with a hook, ready, wearing work gloves. When the boat comes to the side of the lock, I grab the rope with the pole and sit down in the chair with my feet braced on the side of the boat. Good work gloves are important because the rope is slimy. When the boat is at the bottom level, I let go of the rope and grab the pole. Jack by this time has gone back to the driver's seat and slowly drives the boat away. I'm supposed to stop the boat from banging against the wall with the pole. This is how it's supposed to work. We practiced it before we got into the lock. This is not how it happened.

I won't put down all the details, but by the time we got out of the lock, I was on the floor, the pole was broken and one of our bumpers was floating away. By the time I got back on my feet, it was too late to turn around to get the bumper. It would not have done much good if we had, because I think I heard a "pop". Jack was concerned that I had broken a bone (maybe that's what popped) but when he found out I was okay, he started laughing. I was mad at him at first but then when I realized I **was** okay, I chuckled too.

We came into the town of Joliet and tied up at a dock under a bridge to see if we could replace the bumper. The only one they had at the local store was $75! So we walked across the street to a used tire shop and bought 4 old tires for $3 a piece. These are now tied on to the boat with an extra clothes line we brought.

I found a letter from Bill in my bag that he must've stuck in there on Saturday. After reading it I realized just how much I under-estimated that man, and how much I have to thank him for getting me out of there and onto this boat.

I am glad that Jack likes my cooking. It's been a long time since I've had good Indian food, Not that my food is really good. I am enjoying cooking up curry most nights. Probably by the end of the week I'll have had enough of it. It is amazing what memories eating chicken curry brings back.

I am not sure how many miles we made today or what the temperature was, or whether that really matters.

Hudson closed the log book and put it back on the shelf. Jack was just finishing up the dishes from supper.

Ship's Log:
 Day 3
Sept 7, Thursday
We did two more locks today. This time everything went according to plan. I don't know if we are always going to take turns writing in the log, but that's the way it's starting out. Hudson was quiet last night. I thought something was wrong; maybe I'd said something. But when I asked him he told me it was the chicken curry. When I went to get him something for his stomach he said no, it was what he remembered; the problem was in his mind. The

chicken curry tasted like the chicken curry his family had at a restaurant on a trip to New Delhi. They had hired a driver for the day. The driver had come highly recommended, but had sped through an intersection without looking. A car had swerved to miss a cow and had smashed into their car at full speed. He and his wife were okay but their son, David, was badly hurt. As Hudson relived the memory last night it seemed that the pain is still very real for him. His son survived but still walks with a limp today. It's strange how chicken curry brought back the pain of the memory. We talked late into the night about the things that missionaries give up that most people back home do not realize. How sometimes they take on dangers that most people in America can not relate to. We also find joys that most people never find.

We are just beyond the town of Ottawa. There was no dock available so we tucked behind an island in the river and tied up to an old barge that was along the bank.

For supper I made spaghetti with fresh vegetables because we were out of meat. Hudson liked it so much he wanted to make sure I wrote the recipe down: Dice up tomatoes, green peppers, red peppers and a small zucchini that's going soft. Saute an onion in butter and add the rest when the onion is brown. Add lots of oregano, basil and thyme. Serve on noodles and smother in Parmesan cheese.

We are getting low on several supplies. We will have to stop at the next town to stock up. I wish we had one of those wheeled shopping carts. I'll keep my eyes open for a small ice chest. That way we could buy frozen things and keep them for at least a few days.

The next day, Hudson awoke when Jack started the engine. It was barely getting light. By the time Hudson had finished with the bathroom and had gotten dressed. Jack had the boat back in the middle of the river and under way.

"You in a hurry or something?" Hudson asked.

"No, I was up early looking at the map and I'd like to get to Peoria by this evening. There seem to be a few marinas there, and we could stock up on some supplies. Some of these towns look close to the river but when you pass them you realize there's no access if you're on a boat." Jack replied. "Sorry if I got you up too early."

Hudson boiled water for coffee and tea then got out the granola and mixed up some powdered milk. After he handed Jack his coffee Hudson ate his bowl of cereal then took over steering the boat while Jack ate his.

After they had switched places again and the dishes were done, Hudson brought his second cup of tea up to where Jack was and sat down.

After a few minutes of quiet he said, "So, are you going to talk about it?"

"What?"

"You've been so quiet all morning I figured something was on your mind."

After a few minutes Jack said, "What we talked about last night kept me awake and then woke me up again early. How you sacrifice to be on the field; how you give up being around friends and family and having a home in America and you give up your language and what you are comfortable with for the sake of... no, for the privilege of bringing the Gospel to people that haven't heard yet." Jack paused for a minute. "And then when you lose something over there and have to come home, people think you're happier back at home. At least that's the impression I got. But we were happy to give up anything to go and happy to sacrifice anything to be there..." Here Jack stopped, remembering again what he lost. Hudson just waited until he was ready to talk again.

"It sounds strange, but it was a joy to go, even with

81

all that happened I would, no, *we* would do it all again. People think loss is sad. People think holding on to what you have is happiness. But maybe when it comes to the gospel, I don't know, sometimes I don't think it makes sense. Does anything I'm saying make sense to you?" Jack turned to look at Hudson.

Hudson waited a minute before answering. "To me, it makes sense, to most people probably not. You're trying to understand how you can have two apples plus two apples equal three oranges but what you don't realize is that you own the whole fruit stand. Many people can't get their eyes off what they have or don't have to focus on what God has. It's not what you lost or I lost, what I gave up or you gave up that makes us happy or sad. It's whether we are doing what Father God is asking us to do."

I've even met some people on the mission field that were miserable because they thought they would be happy if they went and served, but it was evident that God never called them to go and serve. They were called to stay and send. When they finally accepted this and he went back to this job they found such joy in being able to support those that were called to go. But the opposite is true too, you can stay when you're supposed to go. You found joy in serving in Albania even though you lost your wife, because you were doing what God wanted you to do."

"You're not saying that it was God who killed Sue, are you?"

"Whoa, you're changing subjects, but no, God did not bring you to Albania just to kill Sue and ask you to be happy about it. That gets us into the whole question of God's sovereignty, will, predestination and stuff. That subject is better left for after supper, not just after breakfast. My point is that there is joy in doing what God calls you to do no matter what it costs to do it. Period."

"So why am I happy now? I'm not going, I'm not sending, I'm sailing down the river in a houseboat! What does that have to do with the Gospel?" said Jack, turning again to Hudson.

"You're happy now, because you're doing what God has called you to do, simple." answered Hudson.

It was at this point that Hudson's tea spilled. There wasn't much left in the cup so that wasn't a problem, the problem was the boat was hard aground on a sand bar.

Jack shifted the engine into reverse and revved it up. Nothing moved. He turned the wheel hard to the right then hard to the left, back and forth, getting the boat rocking a bit and slowly it backed away off the sand. It took them just over half an hour to get off the sand bar and back into the clearly marked channel.

After Jack checked the charts and made sure he was in the right place for the third time he smiled and said, "Maybe we'll have to save all conversations till after dinner."

CHAPTER NINE

Late that afternoon they pulled into a marina. After tying up and paying for the night Jack caught a lift with a local to a shopping area nearby. His first stop was a hardware store where he bought a collapsible hand truck, a plastic milk crate, a small cooler and some bungee cords. With these he headed to the local supermarket. He really didn't have a grocery list but knowing what they could and could not fix on the boat shaped his purchases. He picked up a pound of frozen hamburger, two cans of frozen orange juice, and a loaf of frozen bread dough. These would do well keeping other things cold.

Then Jack went for the fresh fruits and vegetables, a dozen eggs, and fresh milk. A few cans of soup and more rice and noodles shaped his dry goods list. The last aisle he went down was the snack aisle. They needed to replace the dozens of cookies and crackers that they ate during the afternoon tea time and coffee break.

After checking out Jack loaded the supplies in the crate and cooler and headed back to the boat. Almost back to the marina, Jack stopped at a convenience store and bought a quart of Ben & Jerry's ice cream.

Hudson had fixed a light supper and had refilled

their water tanks by the time Jack got back. As they sat on the back deck eating their ice cream Jack asked, "Did you gas up the boat?"

"Nope, couldn't bring myself to pay Marina prices for gas when across the street at the local gas station it's almost half the price." answered Hudson. "I figured with that cart of yours you could fill our five gallon cans a couple of times and save a bundle of money."

Jack agreed, although he didn't like the idea of spending his evening hauling gas.

While Jack got the cart ready, Hudson got his two canes out and walked to the convenience store. Jack was tense watching Hudson on the dock, wanting to help. He felt tempted to make him stay in the boat, but he knew Hudson needed to feel independent and wanted to push himself a bit. On the boat Hudson usually sat or was standing by something he could hold on to. It was easy to forget how frail the old man was. But watching him walking on a dock above deep water made Jack nervous.

"What if he fell in?" thought Jack. "Or what if he fell overboard off the back while I was up front and didn't notice in time? Should I make him wear a life jacket or tie a rope to him?" These questions kept Jack's mind occupied while he was filling their gas tank. When he got the boat filled and the two extra cans filled and secured in the back, he went inside and noticed Hudson had not returned. He panicked and wondered if Hudson fell or got lost. Should he call the police? He then realized he didn't have a phone and the Marina office was closed. He jumped back on the dock and almost knocked Hudson into the water.

"Hey, slow down, you're supposed to be on vacation or something like that," said Hudson.

"I didn't know where you were. I thought maybe, you fell or something."

After Hudson and Jack were back on the boat, Hudson turned to him and said, "I can take care of myself, don't worry too much about me, I might surprise you yet."

"Okay, but what took you so long?" asked Jack.

"I bought a phone," said Hudson as he opened the package, "I had them show me how it worked. It has a car jack so I can charge up the battery from the boat's battery and we can stay in touch. You pay by the minute so there was no contract."

Hudson showed him the phone. Jack had not thought of trying to stay in touch with anybody, at least not by phone. The thought was almost novel.

"It works," said Hudson, "I just talked to Bill at home; he says hi."

The picture of Hudson buying and using a cell phone did not fit with Jack's image of him. He'd realized he had always thought Hudson would be behind the times as far as technology was concerned.

"Well I'm going to make use of the marina's showers," said Hudson, "and if you take my hint, you will too."

They also gathered up enough dirty clothes for a load of laundry and had that going while they were showering. It felt good to get clean, but by the time the clothes came out of the dryer it was almost 11:00 p.m.

For the last few days they had not paid attention to a clock. Going to bed when it got dark, getting up when they awoke, eating when they got hungry. So this was a stretch for them both. It was a rude awakening when a lawnmower went off at 7:00 a.m. Glancing out of the front window he saw a crew of men mowing and trimming the small patches of green along the docks.

Unable to go back to sleep with all that noise, he rummaged around in his bags until he found his lap top. He had heard the Marina had wireless Internet service and wanted to check his e-mail. While his laptop was loading up, he made his coffee. It was then that he remembered he was low on coffee. He had enough for another day or two but it meant another stop at another town or walk all the way back to the grocery store.

Jack put off the decision till after his first cup of coffee. With coffee cup in one hand and laptop in the other he went to the forward deck. The server said he had five hundred and thirty-five e-mails. When his spam filter was activated, it went down to one hundred and twenty. By the time he was finished deleting what the spam filter had missed it was only about thirty-five.

It took Jack about an hour to answer what was urgent; the rest he put off answering until the next stop. During the time that he was working Hudson had gotten up. At first Jack thought he was talking to himself but then he realized Hudson was on the phone.

By the time Jack had come back into the boat Hudson was off the phone and was now looking over the maps.

"Do you think we can make it to Havana by tonight?" he asked.

"Sure," said Jack after he had studied the maps and

charts. "Why?"

"Because you're preaching Sunday," came the calm reply.

"What?" said Jack.

"Okay, you've got an adult Sunday school class, or we can do it together. My friend, Bill VanDyke is pastor of the Havana Bible Church. I just got off the phone with him. He says we could tie up at a municipal dock just before this bridge here." Hudson indicated with his finger on the chart. "He'll pick us up there after we give him a call."

"Um..." was all Jack could manage to say.

"Are you worried about speaking?" Hudson asked.

"Well, the last time I was behind a pulpit was at my wife's funeral, and that did not go very well," Jack explained. "I'm an accountant not a preacher. I wouldn't know what to say. I can't very well tell them about going through a lock on the river, can I?"

Hudson paused a minute, and then replied more as a father than as a teacher, "Well, first you pick a Bible verse, then you expound on it a little bit. Then tell a few stories from your experiences and wrap up with a challenge. It may be a challenge to give more, to pray more, to do more or even to go on a short-term or long-term missions trip, but always leave them with a challenge."

Jack thought for a minute. "The only verse that comes to my mind is the 'Go ye therefore' one."

It was obvious by Hudson's face that he was surprised. But then it softened a bit as he replied,

"It's in every book, Genesis to Revelation. Every book of the Bible has at least one theme about missions."

For the next half hour Hudson expounded on his statement, showing that from God's call to Abraham to the marriage supper of the Lamb, each book was pointing towards God's desire to reach the nations.

When breakfast was over, they undid the lines and headed to Havana. It was strange having a deadline, even one that would be very easy to keep. It gave the day's trip a different feel.

After lunch, while Hudson steered for a while, Jack got out his Bible and a notebook and started to work on what he was going to say on Sunday. They agreed Jack would speak for the first fifteen minutes and then Hudson would share for the next quarter hour. Then they would allow for a few questions. Jack thought he could probably find enough to say to fill fifteen minutes.

They pulled into Havana at about 3:00 p.m. At first they were unsure that they had found the right place to tie up. It looked too industrial to be a municipal marina. But as soon as they had their lines secured a tan station wagon arrived.

The driver jumped out and yelled, "Hudson!"

Hudson grabbed his two canes and with a little effort made it onto the dock.

"Bill, good to see you again."

Jack wondered if all of Hudson's friends were named Bill while he went about the boat securing it, turning things off, and locking up. Then he joined them.

"Jack, this is Bill," said Hudson, "Bill, Jack." The two shook hands.

"Bill and I go back about 30 years," Hudson explained to Jack. "The wife and I were traveling around here when our car developed tire problems. Seems you're supposed to rotate them every now and then. Well, I had lost track of how many miles we had been driving and they just plum wore out. There we were stranded, and Bill pulls up noticing our out-of-state license plate. We got a talking and the next thing I know we're spending the night at his house and preaching at his church the next morning. We left Havana with four new tires and a generous offering from the church."

"Lydia has been cooking up a storm ever since your call. I hope you guys are hungry," said Bill as he ushered them to the car.

On the way to his house, Bill gave them the grand tour of Havana. Jack was riding in the back seat listening to the two old friends catch up. From their conversation he could tell that Hudson had visited about every two years, but had kept in email contact far more frequently. Bill even asked questions about the sale of the boat and preparations for the trip.

"First the cell phone and now I see he uses a computer. Hudson is full of surprises!" thought Jack.

After a delightful dinner, they moved to to the living room. Jack had been made to feel part of the family.

"What more have you heard about Yenistan?" Hudson asked Bill.

"Nothing new. Media is just not interested. They would rather report on the Taliban."

They both noticed the blank look on Jack's face.
"It's a new country." explained Bill, "A breakaway country from the old Soviet Union block. We

thought they were all finished, but then up pops Yenistan. We are not quite sure what it will turn into, so we are keeping an eye on it."

The conversation changed course again and again. Jack realized that even though they were in a small town along the river, this pastor was connected to the world. Jack also realized how out of touch he had personally been the last few months.

Soon it became apparent that Bill and Lydia expected them to stay the night. But they had not brought anything with them. Hudson and Jack expected to stay on the boat. It took a while to convince Bill and Lydia that they were quite comfortable in their floating home. Lydia would only let them go back to the boat if she came and gave it her inspection. So the four piled back in the station wagon and headed to the dock.

Jack went ahead to turn the lights on in the boat, while Bill helped Hudson down the dock. Lydia got a flashlight out of her purse to show the way. Jack and Hudson took turns showing off their favorite parts of the boat. Bill was impressed with the engine, the controls and the plumbing for the toilet. Lydia was not impressed, but satisfied enough with the kitchen and the other arrangements that a half hour and a snack at the boat table later, Bill and Lydia drove back home having arranged a time for Bill to pick them up in the morning.

After getting their beds ready and turning off the lights, the two settled into their beds.

Jack heard Hudson roll over and ask, "Are you ready for tomorrow?"

"Wasn't it John Wesley that said you should be ready to preach, pray, sing or die at a moment's notice?"

"Well, are you ready?" asked Hudson again.

"We will see." Then a few moments later Jack asked, "Are all your friends named Bill?"

"We will see." replied Hudson, then rolled over and went to sleep.

CHAPTER TEN

The next morning at the appointed time a different car pulled up to the dock. A man they had never met got out and call to them.

"Mr. Rivers?" the stranger called, "Bill got tied up and sent me to pick you up."

The two got into his car and made small talk on the way to church. The man asked questions about their boat, the type of engine and fuel that they used.

After a cup of unusually good coffee, the adult Sunday school class started. Jack was a little nervous at first but presented what he had prepared. As he got started, he found it easy to share from his heart instead of just his notes. As Hudson suggested he started in Genesis and without realizing it, he used up the full half hour and then some talking about the heart of God for the nations and how central it was to the whole of Scripture. He was surprised when he finished that Hudson stood up and closed with prayer. He then glanced at his watch and realized how long he had talked. Hudson, through half closed eyes, saw the shocked look on Jack's face and smiled.

After the class many people asked both of them questions but on the way up to the sanctuary for the morning service, Jack was able to whisper "Why did you let me go on so long?"

"You were doing good. I couldn't have said it better myself." Hudson replied with a smile.

Hudson got a few minutes to talk in the main service. He greeted several people in the congregation by name and thanked them all for their ongoing support.

After the service, there were more handshakes and hugs and more questions for both of them. Judging from their questions, Jack knew that the pastor shared his global vision with the church.

Lunch was a large affair at the home of the man that picked them up that morning. Several families from the church were gathered around the large table and on couches around the house. They slowly realized that this man was on the board of the church and owned the dock that they were tied up to.

"So, how do you own the municipal dock?" asked Jack.

"It's not the municipal dock. Who said it was?" The man asked back.

"Well, I thought that's what Hudson said. He was

the one that talked to Pastor Bill."

"Oh, that explains it. Bill doesn't get my name right, or at least he pretends not to. You see, my father was half Mexican and gave me the name Manuel, but around here folks just call me Manny. Then my last name, pronounced correctly, is 'Simple'," the man answered emphasizing the last 'e', pronouncing it like in 'a'. "So he probably just said, 'Manny Simple's dock'."

They both laughed at the misunderstanding.

After lunch, Bill and Lydia took them to a grocery store and bought them anything that they thought that they would need for the next few days. When they got back to the boat, they found that one of Manny's crew must have come out and washed the boat and topped off their gas tanks. There was also a basket of fruit placed on the back deck by a family that had known Hudson for years. Leaning up against the cabin door, Jack was surprised to find a brown paper bag with his name on it. Opening up he found a two-pound bag of Starbucks coffee and a note: "I figured you liked good coffee." It was signed, "Manny".

It was with a full boat and full hearts that Jack and Hudson pulled away from Havana the next morning.

After Hudson had joined Jack with his second cup of tea, Jack started asking questions.

"Where did you find a church like that?"

"Havana," laughed Hudson.

"No, I guess I mean, how? How did you find such a mission minded church in the middle of nowhere. You told me about the flat tires but that doesn't tell me how the church got this way."

"It wasn't like this when I first came here. I don't think any church just decides to be a mission-minded church and then goes to look for a missionary. It took about five years before we actually started receiving support from Havana." Hudson shifted his legs and settled down farther into the couch like he was getting ready to tell a long story, so Jack leaned back to listen.

"To grow a mission-minded church, you need to be a church minded missionary," Hudson started slowly. "Part of your job as a missionary is to develop the churches back home, not just plant churches in the field. It's not your main job, but if you forget it you will never be able to do your main job. It's not even like you have two fields you work in, one out there and one back home. Maybe it might seem like that at first, but it should never stay that way. Your vision for your relationship with the

99

church should be something like a team where they handle things on the home front while you handle things on the field. But you have to share the same vision that you are working as one to achieve a common goal."

"We never really thought of it that way," said Jack, "We just signed on with an agency and went where they told us to, spoke at the churches they told us to and left for the field when they said we had enough support."

"Well," said Hudson slowly, "that's one way to do it, but you may not get the prayer support that you do when you're working with individual churches. The churches also do not get a chance to feel closely tied with what you are doing on the field. It wasn't long after they started supporting us that a couple from Havana came to visit us in India. And not just Havana, but several of our supporting churches sent teams of two or three. Once five came. One church made it a point to send somebody to visit us every year that we were on the field."

"Hmm," pondered Jack, "I never thought of my role in developing mission minded churches before. If I ever get back to the mission field, I think I should consider things differently."

"What do you mean 'if'? Haven't you thought of going back on the field?"

"No, it's not that I'm not going to go or planning to go, it's just that I have not given it much thought yet. It's a decision I've put off," explained Jack.

"Hmm..." said Hudson.

Monday night they tied up in Beardstown. Hudson decided to stay on the boat when Jack grabbed his laptop and headed into town to try and find a wireless spot. It didn't take him long as he walked to find a McDonald's that advertised internet access. He ordered a vanilla milkshake and sat at a booth in the corner away from most of the people. As he waited for his laptop to boot up, he scanned the crowd.

How strange North American people looked to him. Young kids lost in video games, teenagers trying to look like they were twenty something, and forty-year-olds trying to look like teenagers. It all made him realize that he was looking at a foreign culture. Could he ever fit in? Could this country ever be home again? But yet, on the flip side, could he ever go back out on the mission field?

This train of thought was interrupted by the e-mails flowing into his in-box. For the next hour Jack weeded and answered. By keeping his replies short, he was able to finally catch up. He briefly checked world news. Other than the major newspapers there were a few websites that Hudson had recommended. He did a search on this new country they mentioned, 'Yenistan'.

Jack did not realize how much time had passed until he realized that the crowd around him had changed two or three times. With guilty pleasure he slurped the last few drops of milkshake from his cup, not caring that he made a lot of noise that when he was younger, got him disapproving looks from his mother. After stuffing his laptop back in his bag, he cleaned up his table and headed back to the boat. As he turned off the main street, he passed by a supermarket and walked in. He really didn't need anything. The folks in Havana had stocked them quite well. He wandered the isles aimlessly until he came to the fruit and vegetables. There he saw them.

"Hudson will love these." he thought, "This must be why God brought me into the supermarket."

After his purchase, he walked back to the boat anticipating what Hudson would say about what was in his bag.

"Ta-da!" said Jack with a grin as he pulled out two mangoes and showed them to Hudson.

"Ugh..." said Hudson with a scowl.

It was not what Jack had anticipated.

"I thought you would've liked mangoes; they're from India!" said Jack, disappointed.

"Sorry, I can't eat them, they disagree with me. And even if I could I don't think I would eat these," said Hudson, turning the mangoes over in his hands. "These are much too green and it looks like the worms have gotten them."

Jack grabbed the mangoes and was about to throw them out when Hudson stopped him.

"Not so fast, I just thought of something, just leave them on the counter," he said.

Jack put away his laptop and mentioned several of the news headlines he had read in an effort to change the subject away from mangoes. As they chatted, Jack unfolded the couch and made up is his bed. He pulled the curtains closed and grabbed the logbook. He filled in the date and the miles, the weather, and since he couldn't think of anything to say he closed the book and put it back on the shelf.

Hudson had left the book he had been reading on the table to go get a notebook from his bag in the back. After a quick search, he then went through his box of spices. He smiled and went back to his first book.

The next morning, after breakfast was over and he

had spent his time with his Bible and hymnal, Hudson went to work on the mangoes. With a sharp knife he peeled and cut them into small chunks and then cooked them up in a pan. As Jack's eyes were on the river he could only guess what all he was doing to them. The smells were incredible. Jack was looking forward to an amazing lunch, so when Hudson served him a tuna fish sandwich he looked at it with a confused disappointment in his eyes.

"It's not ready yet," was all Hudson said over lunch.

The river's current was picking up speed so Jack kept the engines of the boat almost on idle,; just giving it enough to help him steer. There was also more traffic and the wake of the passing barges was getting higher. By the end of the week he thought they should be joining the Mississippi and Missouri River. The thought of their small boat on such massive waterways made him worry. In thinking about taking this trip, he imagined the river would always be like the river they started out on, smaller, calmer. If the barges got any bigger, their wakes could swamp this little boat. It didn't seem designed for such waves. Their engine was strong enough to fight against most currents, but would the current on the Mississippi be too much?

Worry tends to tire a man out. Jack looked for a place to anchor for the night earlier than normal. They didn't need to look for town, nor did they want to. He found a little creek and tucked the nose of the boat up far enough to stay out of the current and the waves on the river. He went to the bow of the boat and tossed their anchor as far as he could. He then put the boat in reverse and backed until he felt the anchor grab the muddy bottom. Satisfied that they would be secure for the night, he turned off the engine and went to the bow of the boat. He sat in a chair facing upstream and began to pray.

"Dear God, You made this river, You made me, You gave us this boat, You called this trip into being. I feel as though I've gotten in over my head in more ways than one. I can't turn back and I don't feel that you are asking me to give up on this trip. I know you have a plan and purpose for all this. I guess all I can say is I trust You more than I can trust myself. Amen."

He grabbed his empty coffee cup and dropped it off in the galley sink as he went on to the bathroom.

As he came out, the thought of music popped into his head. He went over and selected one of his favorite worship CDs and put it in the radio.

Supper was worth waiting for. Jack was surprised when Hudson served up chicken curry. There was one side dish of salad made of cucumbers, tomatoes and green onions. Another bowl contained something that looked like jam. One bite of the curry told his taste buds that Hudson had kicked the spices up a notch.

"Here, try some of this," said Hudson and handed him the jam-like dish.

Jack took a bite and instantly the fire ceased and was replaced with a sweet taste.

"Wow, what is this?" asked Jack as he pointed to the dish.

"Mango chutney."

"Wow," repeated Jack, and tore into the rest of the meal.

Looking around the table he realized Hudson had also made chapattis.

A good meal and good music did a lot to Jack's morale. The chicken curry reminded him that Hudson had had a memory associated with it. Over a desert of cookies and tea, Jack asked Hudson about it.

"It takes an act of the will to replace a painful memory association, with a positive one." Hudson started slowly. "I decided that chicken curry will remind me of the mangoes you bought and our adventures on the river."

"But I thought the mangoes were too bad to eat," questioned Jack.

"Bad mangoes make good chutney," answered Hudson, then he went on, "That's a life lesson I had forgotten."

CHAPTER ELEVEN

They were back to aimless traveling again and it felt good. They had to wait at the lock below Beardstown. When the lock gates opened and the barges pulled up river past them, they realize just how much larger they were getting. Their own boat, which seemed large enough when they started their journey, now looked like a thimble next to these monsters.

They arbitrarily picked the town of Hardin for their next stop. It would be an easy run so they took advantage of extra time and stopped at one of the islands. There were many more of these on the river now. It was a convenient tie up spot to get off the river and rest a bit in the middle of the day. But getting off the boat and onto the island was another story.

Jack was finally able to climb onto a tree branch and down onto the muddy bank. Hudson wisely chose not to follow.

The time wandering around the island gave Jack time to think about the trip ahead. It was changing. He would look out for a small boat to get from boat to shore when they anchored out. Up till now they were able to tie up at docks. Farther down the river the charts indicated that small boat marinas would be fewer and far between.

The trip was changing in other ways too. He couldn't quite put his finger on it. It was more than the fact that the river was getting faster and deeper. It was more than the fact that the barges were getting bigger and the waves rougher.

By the time he got back to the boat an hour had passed. As he was climbing from the tree to the boat he heard Hudson talking on the phone.

"All right Sam, I'll talk to Jack but I think we can do that. We will call again when we get closer... sure, you too... all right, goodbye." Hudson hung up.

"Welcome back," He said as he turned towards Jack.

"What was that phone call about?" Jack asked.

"That was my friend Sam," replied Hudson. "He has a church in south St. Louis. It'd be a nice place to be this Sunday. It's not too far, in fact, we'd have to slow our usual pace down a bit. It's a small church, Anglican, but quite evangelistic … what do you think?" Hudson pointed to the map.

Jack looked at the map, then at the chart, then asked, "Who's preaching?"

"I am," said Hudson.

"Then let's do it," Jack replied.

They did reach Hamlin by that evening. After supper, Jack spent the evening looking at the charts. He was dividing up how many miles they had to go to reach St. Louis by the number of days they had to travel. He made notes on a sheet of paper of interesting places where he would like to pull off. He checked the road atlas for towns to get gas at. He brought up the subject of a small dinghy or some boat that they could carry on top of the cabin and use to get to shore when they weren't tied up to a dock. They decided to split the cost but not go over $100.00.

He checked the St. Louis area charts for a place to tie up, but couldn't find anything listed on the charts for St. Louis proper. There appeared to be plenty of industrial docks and even a casino or two, but no place for travelers. The closest marina was a place just south of town in a little village called Kimmswick. So they set sights on the dock there as Jack finalized the plans.

Jack was up bright and early, eager to set out and launch his plan, but steady rain kept them tied up to the dock. Hudson was content to tidy up the boat and do a few fix up jobs but Jack was antsy. He put on his rain jacket and grabbed an umbrella and made his way to town. He was mad at the rain. He was mad that it upset his plans. He had spent months without plans, and now that he had one, as small as it was, he didn't want it upset. He kicked a stone down the gravel road. It went into the ditch. He kicked an old can down the road. It went into a driveway on his left. Feeling guilty, he picked it up and went across the street to a small store and dropped it in the trash can that was on the front porch.

He went into the store and bought a local paper. There was a small table there with self-serve coffee so he dropped two quarters in the box and grabbed a cup. He blamed the rain for his bad mood. The coffee was not up to the Starbucks he had back at the boat and the fact that there was only powdered cream for the coffee made it worse. He plopped the newspaper on an empty table and turned to the classifieds to look for a small boat. There weren't many ads and all the boats listed were well over $100 but he enjoyed the distraction of looking through this small town paper.

There were ads for Betty's Café, yard sales and the local supermarket, of which there appeared to be only one. The news was mostly who caught the biggest fish and how the local high school team did. He notice the sign by the coffee maker saying, "One free refill." So he filled his cup and just in time heard the clerk say, "The real cream is in the cooler."

Relieved at this blessing he was heading out the

door when he noticed a cork board with hand written advertisements. Mostly, there were free kittens. But there was one on the bottom for a John Boat, listed at $100.00. He borrowed a pen from the clerk and wrote down the phone number.

When the clerk noticed his interest in the boat he asked, "You need a John Boat?"

"Not really, I'm looking for a dinghy for our houseboat," Jack said.

"Well," the clerk drawled, "there is a little red boat out behind the store here that might do. Why don't you take a look at it?"

Jack walked out behind the store where there was a lot more than just a little red boat. It seemed to be a collecting point for a lot of things. There were boat bumpers, large coolers, several bicycles, unidentifiable objects and metal crates. Underneath a tarp, he saw the small red boat poking out. It took him a while to free it from its tangled mess. It was about as long as he was tall and about three feet wide. It had a double wall which would make it unsinkable. Other than being extremely dirty, it looked pretty sound. He went back in to talk to the clerk.

"I might be interested if the price is right," he told the clerk. "How old is it?"

The clerk shrugged and said, "I don't rightly know. It appeared one day after heavy rain. My little bend in the river collects lots of things that float down. What would you say to $50.00?"

"I'd say you've got a deal," said Jack as he reached for his wallet.

After the man shoved the $50.00 into his pocket, he walked out back with Jack. He rummaged through a few other piles and pulled out a couple of paddles that were mismatched but close enough to not make a big difference.

Tossing them into the boat he said, "You'd better take these too, I was ready to haggle down for 30 bucks."

"Thanks." Then Jack added, "I was willing to pay up to $100."

The man laughed, "You must be from Chicago. Nobody around here pays that much for an old boat."

"Well, I was from Chicago, but not anymore," said Jack as he grabbed the paddles with one hand and shouldered the boat on his other side.

"Yeah, where are you from now?"asked the clerk.

"That little houseboat," said Jack, pointing with a paddle to the road that ended at the river where his boat was tied up to a dock.

"Nice place," said the clerk and turned back to the store.

As Jack stepped onto the boat he said, "Seek and ye shall find."

At first Hudson was not impressed, but as he realized that most of the dirt would wash right off and heard the price he had to admit, "God is good."

Jack spent the rest of the morning in a swimsuit, in the rain, cleaning off the boat. When it was clean he hoisted it to the top of the boat and secured it with some bungee cords. The paddles were stuck in a locker in the back.

After lunch the rain had let up enough to let them see down the river they felt safe heading out. The delay has spoiled all his plans and schedule, making them useless, but he had a a nice little boat at a good deal.

Thinking out loud, he said, "You know, if I'd stuck to my plans, I wouldn't have a boat tied up on top." He paused to reflect, "Instead of being mad at the rain I should've been glad."

Hudson did not comment. It was getting close enough to tea time that he put the kettle on the stove and got out the fixings. When the water had boiled he made coffee for Jack and tea for himself. After placing some cookies on a plate in front of Jack and the coffee cup next to it he grabbed his own cup of tea and settled onto the couch.

The tone in Hudson's voice was fatherly as he said, "So you would agree with Scripture when it says 'all things work together for good'...?" He paused for a noisy slurp of his tea, then, chuckling, added, "Well, it's about time."

"I bet you have lots of stories," replied Jack, "about times when circumstances interrupted your original plans only to see that it was God's hand to give you something better."

Hudson smiled and said, "Lots, too many to remember, sometimes I think it's better not to make too many rigid schedules. What you have to do is realize He is sovereign, and don't get upset at upset plans."

They remained quiet, both looking down the river, when Hudson said, "I can't remember who said it, maybe it was on a bumper sticker, but 'Life is what happens when you have other plans'." He then finished his tea and went back to the table.

CHAPTER TWELVE

Ship's log:
Thursday the 14th
We made it to Portage des Sioux. Tied up at the
marina here and while Jack went to find gas for the
boat I was able to walk to a local store and pick up
a few groceries. I can move along pretty good with
my two canes, but I didn't want to try it carrying
groceries, so I used a backpack and kept my
purchases minimal. We did a load of laundry,
although most of the time I've been washing out my
clothes in a bucket on the back deck.

The weather has gotten warm enough to not need
three or four layers in the morning. I'm looking
forward to seeing Sam again. Although this trip is
getting me back in touch with several old friends,
there are many more that I need to reach out to
again. This trip is helping me realize that I'm not
ready for the old folks home. I may have a few
things to give yet.

We have officially reached the Mississippi River. It
rolls. I have to stay seated most of the time while
the boat is underway because of the wake of the
barges and other boats. Jack is doing a good job at
the helm. I talked with a few locals and they say it's
not too much worse until you get farther down the
Mississippi. They think we will be fine until we get to
the Ohio. I had thought of trying to go all the way to

New Orleans but I think that going through the Kentucky lakes and the Tombigbee Waterway may be all that our little boat can handle.

We should make it through St. Louis tomorrow and tie up at Kimswick. That's all for today.

Oh yes. Wind: 5 miles an hour. Temperature: seemed like 80, and since I'm not sure where we anchored last night I have no idea of how far we went today.

Friday the 15th
We finally made it to Kimswick. There's not much here at the marina other than a dock and a lot of old boats. There are a few of us that are going down the river tied up on the river side of the dock. The family behind us is in a million yacht and all I hear between arguments is the game boy and video games of their children. The boat in front of us is a twenty foot sailboat belonging to an eighteen-year-old whose ultimate goal is to circle the world, I hope he gets a bigger boat.

The Marina hardly has a bathroom to speak of so I was wondering what to do about a shower when Jack pulls out a one gallon garden sprayer that he bought in a garage sale when he was working on the boat. He had painted it black and his idea was to fill it in the morning and let the sun heat the

117

water, then pump it up and use it as a shower at night. As it was already evening I heated water on the stove. It worked remarkably well. I sat on the bench on the back deck in my bathing suit and had a good wash. Jack said he wants to hook up a shower curtain back there.

We join the Missouri today and the river is really pushing us fast. Jack has been talking to a few boaters who have made this trip before. They had suggestions about how to get around Cairo and up into the Ohio. It seems like everybody has their own idea. The young man in the sailboat says he might tie up to a barge going that way if he finds one. He says he's gotten a few rides already.

Sunday the 17th
On Saturday morning, Hudson's friend, Sam picked us up and brought us to downtown St. Louis. We did the tourist thing, and went to the museum at the arch. After lunch we headed to the grocery store and stocked up on what we needed. We decided the boat would be all right left alone overnight, so we packed a bag each and went to Sam's house where his wife fixed a glorious supper.

Again the night was filled with talk of missions and world affairs. After a wonderful night sleeping in a bed that wasn't rocking, we went to Sam's little church. It's an Anglican church meeting in a school until they're building gets finished. A wonderful group of people, delightfully mixed. I found the liturgy refreshing. Father Sam had a way of bringing it alive and adding real meaning to it. Hudson did a wonderful job with the sermon. I got to share at the Sunday school class for about fifteen minutes.

After church there was a potluck. It was the first church potluck I've been at that had a cooler of beer. The afternoon stretched on with great fellowship and good conversation. This congregation has a way of making you feel like family.

Father Sam got a call and had to leave for the hospital right away. Somebody was having emergency surgery. A man named Mike was given the responsibility of getting us back to our boat which he did in a roundabout way. After showing us more sites of the city he drove us back to Kimswick. After looking over the boat and asking many questions, he and his wife insisted on taking us to dinner in town. Kimswick, it turns out, is rather historic and has some nice restaurants where everybody dresses in old-fashioned clothing. We sat next to a huge walk-in fireplace that was thankfully not lit.

We should make the bend at Cairo in about three days. We might be able to make it in two if we hurry and get an early start tomorrow.

Part of me doesn't want to hurry. I will be glad to get it over with, but I'm not looking forward to the mix of currents where the Ohio joins the Mississippi. Other boaters tell m there's nothing to be afraid of. Maybe I'm afraid of something else? It is a major milestone, and that means our trip is almost a third over. After this trip I'm not sure what I'm going to be doing. I'd rather just keep floating down the river but rivers always come to an end.

Monday the 18th.
We made it to St. Genevieve and I went for a walk into the town. The road and was a little too far for Hudson so he stayed at the marina chatting with a few other boaters there.

Tuesday the 19th
We made it to Cape Girardeau. There did not appear to be a marina so we pulled into a creek that was just before the town. It was early enough in the evening so I got the dinghy down and decided to try it out. It rowed well and seemed to be pretty stable. Should the two of us need to get in it I think it would be fine. Not that I would trust it on the big river. Tomorrow we round the bend at Cairo.

Wednesday the 20th
We are in Kentucky. Jack had the engines going

before breakfast and was cruising down the river a little faster than normal. I made him an egg and cheese sandwich for breakfast. We only had one close call when a really large barge came around the bend and we had to nip into a small bay to get out of his way. When we got to the actual bend at Cairo, Jack increased the engine speed and cut the curve as close as he could to the Illinois side and headed up the Ohio. We looked for a place to pull in for the night, but everything looked too industrial and full of barges so we ended up tying up to a barge that was half sunk on the Kentucky side of the river. They say this way has a lot less barge traffic, but if that's true I'd hate to see the Mississippi. It seems like all we have around us are barges, some the length of two football fields.

Thursday the 21st
It rained off and on today so we didn't get very far. We also have a lock to go through. There were a few other boats that were anchored along the river so we joined them for the night. We dropped our stern anchor a good way from the bank, then almost ran our bow onto the sandy beach. Jack then jumped off and planted our bow anchor on the shore. We are looking for the turn to go into the Kentucky lakes. Our charts say it's just around the corner and we didn't want to miss it at night.

The next morning the sun was out, and they got a better look at their surroundings. They discovered

121

that they had anchored at Fort Massac State Park. Jack kept looking at the shore over his breakfast.

"Are you okay, Jack?" asked Hudson.

After a few minutes Jack replied, "Yeah sure, it's just..." He got up and went to the bookshelf. Rummaging through a few periodical, he found an old boating magazine that looked well-worn. Flipping through the pages, he stopped halfway through, looked hard at the picture, and then looked hard at the shore.

"I am there," he said softly, and again, "I'm there."

Jack handed the magazine to Hudson and pointed to the picture. Hudson saw the resemblance between the picture in the magazine and the picture out the window of the boat.

"Months ago, before I decided to even take this trip," Jack said, "I was sitting alone in the apartment looking through this magazine. When I saw the people in the picture having fun and the boats tied up to the shore like we are now, I decided that this is what I wanted to do. It was this article, this picture that convinced me to look for a boat. And now I'm here."

Jack was quiet for while, looking sometimes out the window, sometimes at the magazine. Hudson thought he was actually looking inside, trying to figure out an emotion. After several minutes, Jack started the engines, and hauled in the bow anchor. Hudson went to the back and hauled in their stern anchor. Then they were off again.

Hudson broke the silence, "You didn't want to just stay there?"

"It was a goal, but now that I have reached it, why stay there? What good is a goal, if once you reach it you stay there and don't move on?" Jack paused and was quiet for a while. "I want to see these lakes. They say they're very beautiful, and besides, winter is coming and Florida is warmer."

Hudson had a sense that turning the bend in Cairo and coming to that beach was turning a corner in Jack's life and reaching a point from which he could go on. It seemed to indicate a look towards the future more than a dwelling on the past.

CHAPTER THIRTEEN

They rolled on past Paducah and found the canal that led to the chain of lakes in Kentucky. To the right and left they saw many barges tied up. There were also several boats heading in their direction. Hudson recognized a family that he had met in Cape Girardeau and went to the forward deck to wave at them. Just then they hit wake and Hudson nearly tumbled into the water.

Coming back into the cabin Hudson brushed it off as no big deal, but it renewed a concern for Hudson's safety in Jack. Yes, he was getting stronger, yes he was able to do more and more, but he was still an old man that not too long ago was in the nursing home with a broken hip. Was Hudson honest with how he was feeling and how he was getting along? Or was Hudson just pretending so that Jack would keep taking him down the river? He realized he'd been more focused on getting around the point at Cairo than keeping track of how Hudson was doing. These should be calmer waters, but still Jack promised himself to keep a better eye on Hudson.

Later that day they made it to the lock into the Kentucky lakes. They had to wait for several boats that were coming up river before they got a chance to proceed.

After being on rivers for so long the lake seemed huge. There was no current, first of all. Then also they didn't have to follow the charts from buoy to buoy, they could just point and go.

Hudson had contacted some friends that lived down towards the end of the lake. It was a couple that he had worked with in India. They had a small cottage on a bay somewhere down near Cyprus Creek.

Jack realized that with no current they would be using more gas, so before they got too far in they pulled into a Marina at Grand Rivers and filled their tanks. They had enough food for a while so they decided to continue on and anchor someplace that evening. But before pulling away from the gas station they each had an ice cream cone to celebrate making it to the lakes.

The cove that they chose was beautiful, with the sun setting over the lake, but the scene that greeted them in the morning took their breath away. The sun was just touching the shore on the opposite shore when they got up. Mist was gently rising like a blanket being pulled off the sleeping ducks. Both of them just sat and watched it, drinking it in along with their morning coffee and tea.

It was almost noon when they finally started the engines and pulled up the anchor It was wonderfully calm. Apart from a few other boats that stayed well away from them, they were alone. Hudson took the helm for a few hours, insisting on wearing the baseball cap Jack had, calling it the captain's hat. Jack noticed that Hudson was trying to get around the boat without much assistance. In this calmer water, he could just about do it. Jack did not let himself forget about the stumble on the front deck, however, and maintained his vigilance for him.

Jack took a turn at making the tea and serving it to Hudson as he steered. When he had had enough Hudson went back and sat on his bunk. Jack wondered if something was bothering him, but figured Hudson would bring it up on his own.

Besides, he was having too much fun driving the boat down the middle lane of the lake. Therefore it was quite a surprise and shock when he heard a cry and a splash.

Slamming the engine into reverse brought the boat to a sudden stop. Jack turned off the engine and ran to the back deck. Grabbing a life jacket that he had put there for just this type of emergency, he looked around to see where Hudson had gone in. The only thing that he could see was the disappearing form of Hudson's walker sinking slowly beneath the water. He was ready to jump in with a life jacket when Hudson's hand on his arm prevented him.

"I wouldn't do that if I were you. The water's awfully cold," said Hudson calmly.

"But... you...," stammered Jack, pointing to the now disappearing walker.

"I'm okay, and I'm sorry if I scared you. You almost did knock me overboard when you stopped the boat so suddenly," said Hudson.

Jack sat down on one of the chairs and started to breathe again.

Hudson sat down on the other chair. "I had better explain. I know I should not have thrown the stupid thing overboard. I'm sorry I've polluted this beautiful lake. But I'm tired of having that useless thing hanging around. It made me think I was a cripple, or an old man, or something." He laughed. "I also wanted to baptize it." Hudson paused and studied the look on Jack's face. "In baptism you have death and resurrection. I needed to do something to show that the old Hudson, the one you found sitting in a nursing home in a wheelchair, does not exist anymore. I think when we rounded the bend at Cairo, and tied up at that beach, you had a bit of change in your attitude too, didn't you?"

He waited till Jack nodded.

"Well, God has been talking to me, and he's not done with me yet. And he's not done with you either. We both have important things to do, and we cannot let our past tell us what limits are to be on our future. I think today I have a greater understanding of the Bible verse, 'I can do all things through Christ who strengthens me.' Now, let's find a nice place to anchor, we've got to make some pizza for supper.

But Jack did not move yet. He was trying to take in everything that Hudson had said. The words, 'not finished', and 'important things to do' kept going around in his mind. He gradually processed most of what he said, but when he got to the pizza part there was something about it that didn't make sense. They had no oven.

When he finally came to his senses, Hudson had started the engines and was heading down the lake. Jack walked up to him and simply asked, "pizza?"

"Check the cooler."

Jack walked back down to the galley and looked at the cooler. The top was being pushed open by rapidly rising bread dough that he had forgotten they had purchased. Hudson had made the first batch of frozen bread dough into flatbread in the frying pan. So the last time they went shopping he had picked up another batch, but he had forgotten it, and now here it was rising rapidly, ready to overflow out of the cooler.

"But how?" was all Jack asked.

"Would you come back up here and steer? Let me figure that out." Jack complied.

Glancing over his shoulder from time to time, he watched as Hudson kneaded the dough back into shape, then, flattening it out with a rolling pin, he placed it in the large cast iron skillet. He put the flame on very low and put the lid on. Fresh-made bread smells started to fill the boat. About 10 minutes later he flipped the bread over and covered it with cheese, tomato sauce and some sliced pepperoni. They he sprinkled it with a multitude of herbs. Sensing that supper would be served soon, Jack looked for a place to anchor.

By the time Jack had secured the anchor and had turned off the engines, the pizza was served.

"Not bad, not bad at all," said Jack.

"Well," said Hudson in between bites, "when you're a missionary, you have to figure out how to make do with what you have."

That evening, Jack rummaged around and found

enough fishing tackle to piece together something he could fish with. Early in the morning he was able to catch a few bluegill and a perch using pieces of leftover pepperoni as bait.

By the time Hudson was up and about, the fish fillets were browning nicely in the pan. After breakfast, Hudson as usual, grabbed his hymnal and Bible and opened it up to his daily reading schedule.

"Hey, it's Sunday," he said.

Jack, who had also lost track of days, took a while to think this through.

"So who's preaching today?" Jack finally asked.

"Let's just take the day off, this is a nice bay. I wouldn't mind trying my hand at fishing. We could take a dip in the lake, maybe I'll even get that boat off the top of the cabin and paddle around a bit. What do you say?"

"You will get no arguments from me," answered Jack.

Jack got the dinghy down from the top and got out the oars. With a little help Hudson was able to get in and he took off.

Jack sat on the back of the boat and read a book, trying to not be concerned about Hudson's safety.

Sometime later, the lake looked just too good to pass up and Jack dove in. The water was almost too cold, but it was an enjoyable swim anyways. By the time Jack was dried off, Hudson was back from his paddling about and they had a cup of tea. The rest of the day was spent fishing, reading or taking naps.

It was really the first time they had just relaxed for a whole day. Not that steering a boat was hard work but it did keep you busy. Hudson concocted a supper of fried fish with curry and onions. They commented on how much they enjoyed that day.

"Didn't you ever take a day off in Albania?" asked Hudson.

"Once a month maybe, if that." said Jack. "There seemed to always be so much to do."

Hudson gave him one of his fatherly looks. "So you think God was joking when he said to honor the Sabbath?"

"No, we were in church every Sunday."

"And was it restful?"

"No," Jack said slowly, "it was probably the busiest day of our week."

"'Sabbath', means rest. Let me ask you a question, would you have funded your ministry by robbing a bank?"

"No," Jack answered slowly not sure of what Hudson was getting at.

"Then why do missionaries feel justified in breaking another one of the Ten Commandments just for the sake of getting a few more things done?"

Jack said nothing, but was relieved that Hudson's focus now was on missionaries in general, and not on him specifically.

"It was the hardest thing for us to do, to get people on our team to take a day off. Friday, Saturday, Sunday, it didn't matter. We wanted them to take one day out of seven to honor God by resting. If I hear one more person say that they just want to burn out for God rather than rust out, I think I'll slap them. Our bodies were made to take a day of rest. It's an act of faith, trusting that God will see that things get done. It's an act of tithing your time."

Jack wisely just nodded affirmation and let Hudson continued his rant.

Hudson got up and began pacing back and forth quoting Scripture, making his points with his fork still in his hand.

"Promise me," he said in conclusion, "that when you're back on the field you will take a day off *every week*!"

Jack noticed that Hudson did not say 'if' you get back to the field, but 'when'.

After they cleaned up supper dishes, they got out the charts and plotted their course.

"George and Martha live about here, and if we push it we can make it in a day but I would suggest that we take our time and show up there sometime Tuesday. What do you think? asked Hudson.

"Or even Wednesday," answered Jack. "Look at all these bays, it might be fun poking in a few of them."

So Hudson got out his cell phone and called his friends. They chatted for a while in Hindi, then Hudson motioned for a pad of paper and a pencil and started scribbling some things down, numbers and letters that at first didn't make any sense to Jack.

"Okay, we'll keep an eye out. Thanks for the information, and call if you find out anything new."

And Hudson closed the phone.

He went back over to the charts and studied them for a while.

"How about if we make it here by tomorrow night?" he said. "It seems like a well protected bay."

"Okay, fine with me, but why are you interested in a well protected bay?" asked Jack.

"Because were going to have to ride out the hurricane."

"What?" Jack said with surprise.

"Well, the remains of what was a hurricane. It should be passing through here day after tomorrow. We could expect a lot of rain and wind. It might put us off schedule a day or so." explained Hudson.

They both suddenly realized how unconnected with current news they really were. Jack turned on the radio and found a news station that gave them a few updates before they went to bed.

The next day the sky was noticeably grayer. They found the bay Hudson had suggested and put out both anchors, testing them to make sure they were holding well. They took in anything that was loose. The two chairs in the back were hooked to the railing with bungee cords. They really didn't know what else to do to get ready for the storm other than keeping an ear to the radio for updates. Where else could they go? What else could they do? They couldn't climb into the basement, or go to a shelter. They felt a little helpless and vulnerable.

The mood only changed when Hudson walked over to the radio and put in Jack's favorite worship CD.

The storm hit at 3:16 a.m. Jack knew this because that was what the clock said when it got knocked off the shelf and hit him across his nose.

"What was that?" asked Hudson when Jack yelled.

"My clock, it got knocked off the shelf and fell on my nose."

"Time flies when you're having a hurricane," chuckled Hudson.

Jack got up and inspected the damage done to his nose and was relieved to see it wasn't bleeding. He tried to look out the windows to see what was happening around them but the sky was too dark.

"It's been going on for about an hour," said Hudson. "There was a bit of hail not too long ago, we might have lost one of our chairs off the back."

Even though the bay gave them some shelter from the wind's force, they could hear the strain on the anchor lines. Neither of them could get back to sleep. Neither of them could read in that rocking boat. Jack busied himself with checking to make sure nothing else was loose and could get knocked off a shelf or rolled around in a cupboard. Then for several hours they laid on their beds feeling the weight of the storm around them. About 6:00 a.m. they decided to just get up.

The creaking of the boat and their anchor lines mixed with the howling of the wind and the sound of the rain made it hard to carry on even simple conversations. Neither of them felt like eating much breakfast. At 7:00 a.m. it was light enough that Jack wanted to go check the lines. In his bathing suit he went first forward then aft. Out back he untied the anchor line and let out about another foot or so. Then he went forward untied the anchor and pulled it in a foot or so. He then grabbed some rags and wrapped them around the anchor lines where they were rubbing against the boat. Hudson guessed Jack must feel secure in how the boat was holding up when he saw him grab a bar of soap and take a shower in the warm rain of the hurricane.

Just as he got in and dried off, the wind shifted. This new, sudden tug caused the bow anchor line to snap. Jack held on as he felt the boat swing 90°. With the sound of a crunch he realized the bow was now resting in the branches of a tree that had been knocked into the lake earlier. With their back door now facing the brunt of the wind and the rain, water was finding new ways of seeping into the boat. Jack watched as small rivers came through the window cracks and through the floorboards.

"Bilge pumps!" he shouted and went to the control panel and flipped the switch. Nothing happened. Opening up an access panel, Jack saw that the water level in the bilge was getting close to six inches. Hudson, without a word, started working the hand pump while Jack looked for the loose connection to the electric pumps. Tracing the lines back from the pumps he realized it was only a blown fuse. Unable to find a new fuse with the correct amp, he simply used a paper clip to turn them on. Thankfully they started working.

With things somewhat under control they both went back to their bunks. Exhaustion from lack of sleep and panic help them to doze off and on.

By three in the afternoon, the rain had let up a little, and Jack and Hudson had a normal lunch.

By five the rain was down to a drizzle and they could step out back and survey their world. The broken line from their bow anchor was floating about 50 yards away. Their bow was nestled in a tree closer to shore than where they had anchored the previous day. Both chairs were gone and their anchor light was smashed.

"When the bow line broke, we must have dragged the stern anchor a ways before it reset itself," said Jack.

"Just in the nick of time, looks like," observed Hudson, looking at the branches entangled in their bow.

"I'm worried about the hull," said Jack, "I heard a bump last night; I think we hit a log."

Hudson grinned sheepishly, then said, "That was me, I fell out of bed."

"What? And you laughed about my clock?"

When they stopped laughing, Jack started the engine, mostly just to make sure that it would still run. They ended up pulling in their stern anchor and heading out to rescue their bow anchor. Motoring around their now cluttered bay, they searched for their lost chairs. Around a corner there were two chairs, but they were hunter green. With the boat hook, Hudson managed to get them on board.

"The Lord gives and the Lord takes away..." he said. Jack replaced the broken line on the anchor and they anchored for the night in a sandy spot in a more open part of the lake.

By evening the stars were out. They sat on the back deck breathing in the freshly cleaned air.

Hudson went in and grabbed the ship's log. Coming back out with a pen, he simply wrote: September 27, stormy, didn't go anywhere but up and down.

Handing the book to Jack he asked, "Do you want to add anything?"

"Nope, that says it all." Jack responded when he read it and handed the book back to Hudson.

CHAPTER FOURTEEN

The next morning, Hudson called his friends and assured them that they made it through the storm. There were very few boats abroad that day. Whenever they were close to a shoreline they had to watch out for branches that were floating in the water.

Over lunch, Hudson talked about his friends George and Martha. They had several children, some of whom they had adopted. Hudson wasn't sure who would be in the house. Jack was looking forward to meeting yet more new friends of Hudson's. They kept praise and worship CDs on most of the day, only occasionally tuning in to the radio to find out news about the weather. The radio indicated they had seen the last gasp of the dying storm. It was now little more than intermittent rain.

Jack eased the throttle forward a little, trying to get to the bay before the sun set. Hudson was standing at the table looking at the road atlas and the lake charts. Every now and then he would point out a landmark to Jack. Finally he pointed to an inlet and said, "There it is."

He then got out Jack's laptop and found the picture from the e-mail his friend's had sent. Steadying himself with one hand and holding the laptop with the other he made his way up to where Jack was steering the boat.

"That's what we're looking for, should be on the right here someplace soon," said Hudson, and then they were both quiet, looking at the shoreline passing by.

After about twenty minutes, Jack pointed to a dock fifty yards ahead and asked, "Could that be it?" After a few minutes a sign saying, "Welcome Hudson and Jack" was visible on the railing.

After tying up the boat, they made their way up to the cottage that was nestled among the trees on the small rise up from the lake. It had a screened in front porch that gave a picturesque view of the small bay. Halfway up the walk, they were noticed by somebody inside. They could hear happy voices saying things like, "They are here!" and other things in a language Jack could not recognize.

Soon they were inside a small living room, and Jack was being introduced to George and Martha Hamilton. Hudson was being plied with questions, and both of them had to expound on the storm. Just then Jack was startled by a third voice calling them to supper. As they made their way into the large eat-in kitchen, Jack saw a young Indian lady just putting a pot of soup on the table. She was dressed casually in jeans and a T-shirt and her evidently long black hair was tied up in a bun.

"Ruth, it smells delicious, thank you," said George.

"Kokila, it is so good to see you again!" said Hudson beaming at her.

To this the young lady smiled and put her hands together, bowed, and said, "Namaste, Uncle Hudson." Then she went over to him and gave him a hug and a kiss on the cheek.

George spoke up, "Jack, this is our daughter, Ruth, also known as, "Kokila". Ruth, this is Hudson's friend, Jack." To this, Kokila again put her hands together, bowed and said 'Namaste' to Jack.

Over dinner, Hudson got caught up with George and Martha. The talk was a lot about India and occasionally slipped into Hindi, but not wanting Jack to feel left out, they kept it mostly in English. The boat trip, where they had been, and where they were going also featured in discussions.

The soup and fresh hot bread was delicious. Jack and Hudson had seconds, but Jack noticed the other three were not eating much. Dessert was fresh sliced peaches served over a large scoop of vanilla ice cream.

After dinner they moved back to the living room. George and Martha eased into overstuffed chairs. Hudson and Jack sat on the couch facing them.

Within minutes Kokila came out with sweet milky Indian tea. After serving each one, she took her cup and sat down on a chair that she had brought in from the kitchen.

"Kokila, this is the best tea I've had since I have had to leave India," said Hudson affectionately.

"Thank you Uncle, if you would like I can prepare an Indian meal for you tomorrow night." Then turning to Jack she asked, "Do you like Indian food, Jack?"

"Yes, I've come to love it. Hudson fixes it quite often," said Jack, to which George and Martha started laughing and almost could not stop.

"Hudson, fixing Indian food?" George and Martha said together in between fits of laughter. "No, whatever Hudson fixed," they said to Jack, "was definitely not Indian food."

When the laughter had died down, Hudson offered, "If you will fix me an Indian meal, Jack and I will prepare lunch on our boat and we could bring it up to the picnic table there." he said, pointing just outside.

Everyone thought it was a wonderful idea and with the plans made, Hudson stood up.

"Well, we better turn in for the night," he said, and after good nights all around they made their way back to the boat.

As they were getting into their bunks, Jack said, "George and Martha seemed like a real nice couple..."

"But..." offered Hudson, noticing a question in Jack's voice.

"It seems their daughter is more of a servant." observed Jack.

Hudson paused before he answered. "George and Martha were on the field long before we got there. They taught us a lot from their experiences. I've lost track of how old they are, maybe ten years or so older than I am, and Calcutta was not a healthy place to live. I'm surprised they have lasted this long. So they do need a lot of help just to get up in the morning and go to bed at night. But I have to disagree with you, they do not treat their daughter like a servant. They have never asked her to do anything for them, she has chosen to do it. She is a very well educated young lady, George and Martha saw to that. She speaks several languages and continues to travel back to India with short-term mission trips and other groups." Hudson paused, "why don't you ask her, sometime tomorrow, why she treats them like she does?" Then he rolled over and went to sleep.

The next morning Jack borrowed the Hamilton's car and drove into town to pick up some fresh supplies. Several of the things that he bought he placed in their freezer. He was only allowed in the kitchen briefly, for supper preparations were already begun. Now he knew why Hudson offered to make lunch. Pieces of chicken and vegetables and other unidentifiable things were scattered around the kitchen, each item either cooking or marinating or waiting to be washed. Kokila, was humming a happy Indian tune as she ruled over the kitchen like a conductor over an orchestra. Jack wanted to just sit and watch her work, but this was not allowed.

Jack and Hudson took the opportunity to clean up the boat a bit, inside and out. Jack found a new light bulb for their anchor light but as the cover was smashed he ended up taping a plastic cup over the bulb to protect it.

For lunch they served grilled sandwiches from some of the ingredients that Jack picked up that morning; fresh thinly sliced red and green peppers, sweet onions, Monterrey Jack cheese and thin slice deli ham that was on sale at the local Piggly Wiggly. There was almost a fourth of July feeling to their picnic. They had even brought out lemonade and served watermelon for dessert. But again the three Hamilton's ate sparingly.

The afternoon passed quietly, with George and Martha even taking naps. But if Jack wanted to talk with Kokila, she was either too busy in the kitchen or busying herself with taking care of the house.

Just before supper, Hudson called Jack over. "If you're going to have an Indian meal we had better get dressed for it," and handed Jack an Indian style shirt that he had borrowed from George. "Try this on."

While Jack did that, Hudson changed into an Indian outfit that he had obviously brought with him.

When they made their way back up to the cottage the aromas coming from the little house were incredible. They noticed that the kitchen table had now moved to the living room and was draped with a fine tablecloth with an Indian print. But the design was lost under many serving dishes with an array of colors and smells that Jack had never seen or sensed before.

George and Martha were already seated and dressed in appropriate Indian outfits.

"You men look wonderful," said Martha, motioning to the table, "please sit down, Ruth is just bringing the last dish and then we can start."

Just then, Ruth came in carrying a platter of

chapattis. She was dressed in a fine, pale blue silk sari. Her long black hair was loose down her back and intertwined in it was a string of small white flowers. Jack thought he had never seen anyone so beautiful.

Throughout the meal, Kokila acted more as hostess. She explained every dish to Jack, showing him how to use his chapatti to eat with. Jack noticed everyone was using a fork and knife except her.

"Indian food always tastes better when eaten with your hand." she explained.

At the end of the meal George turned to Jack and asked, "Now, you have had a real Indian meal, is it anything like Hudson has ever made for you before?"

"With all due respect to Hudson, I can honestly say, that compared to what I have just eaten, Hudson's food is closer to cardboard," he said with a smile.

Even Hudson laughed.

"Indian food is what God created our mouths to taste. Anything less does not take full advantage of the taste buds God created us with," said George.

When Kokila stood up and started to gather the

dishes, Hudson stopped her.

"No, I can get started on the dishes. You've done enough work for a while. You haven't even seen our boat." Turning to Jack he said, "Jack, why don't you give Kokila a little tour of our humble home."

"I'd be delighted to," said Jack and got up and opened the door for her.

Jack noticed, on the walk to the boat that the rustle of her sari matched the rustle of the wind in the trees. Helping her onto the boat, he saw that she was barefoot and she had her ring on her toe. He gave her a brief tour. Thankful they had cleaned the boat that morning.

"It is a little cramped," he said, "but we do alright."

She smiled and said, "In India two families would live in this space."

On the back deck, she stood and admired the view of the water.

"If it's okay, I'd like to ask you a question," said Jack, motioning for her to sit in one of the chairs.

Sitting, she asked, "What would you like to know?"

"Well maybe I should just ask, how did you become

a Hamilton?"

She stared at the water for at least a whole minute.

"My mother was a prostitute," she began, "my father, judging from my light skin, was either an American or European. When my mother was pregnant with me, George and Martha started to reach out to her, helping her with food and vitamins. Without their help I probably would not have survived."

After I was born, my mother went back to work, but she started to believe in Jesus. When the madam found out, they beat her and made her work longer hours. Early in the mornings, she would sing to me quietly what she called her Jesus songs. Songs she had learned from George and Martha."

By the time I was three, it was obvious my mother was dying, probably from AIDS. George and Martha did what they could, but my mother lasted only another three years. Close to the end of her life, George and Martha took us into their house to care for her. She died when I was six, and my mother had just turned twenty. That was thirty years ago."

Somehow, my mother had been able to sign papers that gave George and Martha the right to adopt me. It almost didn't happen though. The madame said my mother still had a debt that I would have to work to pay it off. She said because of my fair skin I could fetch a high price. I don't know where they got the money, but George and Martha paid the debt. They changed my name to Ruth and moved to a different part of the city." she paused. "Does my story shock you?"

"What shocks me is that this could have happened. That. There are people, even children, being bought and sold in our world today."

"Not only could it happen, it has happened for thousands of years. It is happening today in ever increasing numbers."

"I can see why you love them and serve them like you do."

"Not quite," she contradicted politely, "I do what I do for them, not just for what they did for me, but because of what they have done for over forty years of service to countless hundreds of people like me. I consider it an honor to serve them because I know that in Calcutta today there is a church of well over three hundred people that would not be there if it had not been for them. They gave of their lives for the gospel and it is because of the gospel that I serve them. Do not think that I am trying to pay back a debt that I owe them. It's more because of my love for Jesus that I serve them."

They were both quiet for a while, then changing the subject she smiled and turned to Jack asking, "How is Uncle doing?"

Jack explained about Hudson's hip surgery and recovery and how he was getting stronger. He realized as he talked about it, that it had been a while since he had seen Hudson use both canes. She seemed quite pleased at his progress.

"Well I had better go and help them finish up the dishes," she said and stood to leave.

He climbed to the dock and offered his arm to help her up. She accepted his offer, and kept hold of his arm all the way back up to the house. Just before going inside she turned to him and said, "Take good care of Uncle for me please."

"I'll do that, I promise."

Back in the house they found the dishes done and the three of them talking in the living room. The kitchen table was still there so Jack and Hudson moved it back to the kitchen. Then the five of them sat down with tea and talked late into the night.

Hudson waited until they were both in bed until he asked Jack, "Well, did you ask her your question?"

"She has an amazing story. What is really

interesting is that I've noticed she almost carries herself with a sense of royalty, but she has chosen a job of service. She truly knows she is the daughter of the most high King even though her mother was a prostitute. And why does she call you Uncle? She seems to care for you a lot."

"'Uncle' is a term of affection in India, but in her case you could say I really am an uncle. When George and Martha adopted her, they talked to us about caring for her should anything happen to them. So if George and Martha should die, I become responsible for Kokila."

The next morning after breakfast, they make plans to leave. Jack brought the charts in from the boat and showed them their plans for the Tennessee Tombigbee waterway, followed with Florida. Jack exchanged e-mail addresses with Kokila and they promised to stay in touch. He remembered at the last minute the things he had put in their freezer.

After their goodbyes, they sadly pulled away from the dock. Later that night Jack found the Indian shirt he had worn for the banquet.

"Oh no, I thought I had returned this." he said, holding it up.

"You did, George wanted you to have it, sort of to remember your visit and your first real Indian meal."

CHAPTER FIFTEEN

That day they made it past New Johnsonville. It looked mostly industrial along the river. They were calling it a river again even though technically they were still in the Kentucky lakes. So they went on to a place called Sycamore Landing. It turned out to be little more than a sandy place to drop an anchor.

After a leisurely breakfast they decided to go ahead and travel a bit more, even though it was Sunday. Hudson found a Christian radio station that was broadcasting some church's Sunday morning sermon. The pastor had chosen the passage; "my house shall be a house of prayer..." and it was a pretty good sermon on prayer. But Jack missed something.

"What happened to the part ... 'for all nations?' What about the call to world evangelism that's so evident in that passage?"

"Because the hand is not a foot, it should be cut off?" asked Hudson.

Jack spun his head around at this comment and stared at the Hudson. "The only way I can make any sense out of your comment is to attribute it to the fact that you might be getting senile." he said.

Hudson laughed. "That's because you're still just a

foot!" he said. Then he explained. "If you look at the body of Christ, Christ is the head, of course. The way that I see it, missionaries are the feet. It talks about 'blessed are the feet of those who bring good news' and 'have your feet shod with the gospel of peace'. Therefore if we talk about the feet as being the missions of the church, we might as well say that the hands are the praying part of the church. There's a lot that goes on in the body of Christ other than just missions. But just like a body cannot run without feet, a body can't feed itself without hands. So just because this pastor is paying attention to another part of the body, it doesn't mean he's wrong. I think sometimes the local church janitor has as much a role in the body of Christ as a missionary on the front line."

"Okay, what about the lady that organizes the potlucks, and makes sure that there is green bean casserole?" asked Jack.

"It's not necessarily the role that's either important or unimportant, but it's how the person sees their gift and if they are using their gift to bless the whole body. It's whether they see themselves as a servant or whether they are looking for praise. It's more in the attitude than in the job."

"So maybe a janitor with a servant's heart, is more productive than a pastor or missionary without one?"

"I think both are more valuable than a boat captain that's not watching where he's going," said Hudson.

"Huh?"

"Tree branch."

Jack was able to turn fast enough that the branch only scratched against the side.

They pulled into a town called Clifton where they docked at a marina for the night. Hudson tried to make a green bean casserole for supper.

"If you make this again," said Jack, "I will throw you overboard for sure."

The next day they checked in the marina store for a new anchor light, but they found nothing that would fit their boat, so the plastic cup stayed. As they continued traveling, they switched off driving every few hours.

"So what is the next goal?" asked Jack, when he took over driving from Hudson.

"Mobile, Alabama." answered Hudson, "Unless that answer does not fit your question, in which case the answer could be: save the world, stay alive, round that next bend or even get you back on the mission field. Now which answer fits your question?"

"I did not mean for it to be so complicated, but I guess all those answers fit my question. I don't know, but maybe sometime soon I'll be ready to start looking at what's after this trip for me. Do you ever think about what you're going to be doing when we get to Florida? I mean, are you going to play golf all day? Or are you more the shuffleboard type?" asked Jack.

"Oh, I've got plans, I don't think you need to worry about how I'm to spend my days. How about you? Have you given any more thought to going back on the field?"

"Some," he answered. "It would probably be a little different than the last time I went."

"How so?" asked Hudson.

"Well, I would have a better support group back home, for one, and then have plans in place in case of emergencies. Then I think a lot of the other changes would just be in my attitudes." answered Jack thoughtfully.

"Well of course it's going to be different," answered Hudson. "Every place you go is going to be different. New places require new attitudes and plans and ways of doing things. Take for instance this 'Yenistan'. It used to be part of Russia so most of the people will speak Russian but it's background has been Muslim so roughly sixty percent, would not consider themselves Russian Orthodox. They may even try to resurrect some tribal languages that have been long lost since the takeover. Are you going to treat it as a Middle Eastern country or a western country? Whatever you do there is going to look different from any other outreach done in any other country."

Jack was quiet, thinking about what Hudson had just said. "Why are you so interested in Yenistan?"

"I have a few friends that are putting together a team from different agencies. They'll be heading over trying to do some church planting within a month or two," said Hudson.

Jack was quiet the rest of the day.

They were able to get past the town of Savanna, Tennessee. A quiet cove where they could anchor for the night was waiting behind an island.

The next morning as Hudson was starting his quiet time and Jack was putting on the kettle, Hudson looked up and asked, "What day is it?"

Jack checked the log book and realized they had not written in it for a while. He looked at the calendar, but couldn't figure out from that to be certain. So he finally opened up his laptop and checked.

"Today, is Tuesday, October 2," answered Jack confidently. "Why?"

"Because today, Tuesday October 2nd, Hudson Taylor Rivers, turns 72 years old."

"Wow! You didn't tell me. I have no presents. So what do you want to do for your birthday?"

"I really have not thought about it. I suppose I should celebrate somehow. We can't really invite friends over for supper, let's see, where do we start?"

"We'll start with breakfast. What would you like for me to fix for you?" asked Jack.

Hudson thought for a minute then smiled and asked, "How about a cheese omelet, fried potatoes and some toast?"

"I think I can manage that," said Jack as he reached in the cupboard and pulled down a can of potatoes. He got out both frying pans and got the fire going under each one. In the large one he put some butter and started the potatoes frying, In the other one he placed buttered bread. While both of these were going, he scrambled up some eggs and grated some cheese. His cooking skills were improving. He was now throwing in more spices, learning from Hudson to, as they say, "kick it up a notch."

Soon breakfast was ready and served. Hudson took his time enjoying everything. While Jack was washing the dishes he asked, "So, what would you like for lunch?"

Hudson was ready this time and without any pause or hesitation answered, "A hot dog and a Klondike bar. And for supper I like to do some fishing and fry up some fresh fish."

"Well you check the charts and see if we have a town coming up, and we'll just see if we can get you that."

What they found was that they were leaving the Kentucky lakes and entering into the Tennessee River. This was a little confusing at first because the lakes had become little more than a canal and the Tennessee River after Pickwick Dam looked more like a lake. After they cleared the lock, they pulled into Pickwick Landing State Park. Several kids ran down to the dock and caught their lines. Their family was having a picnic at the park. After getting them tied up the usual questions started. "Is this your dad? How far did you come? You're really living on this boat?"

159

Hudson had a few questions for them, the main one being, "How is it that you are not in school?"

"We homeschool. We finished up early today and mom said we could have a picnic ... and the little kids had just finished studying about locks ... and I was studying about shipping methods ... and it was a nice day ..." said several voices all at once.

Hudson at once started quizzing them as to who made the dam and why. The kids seemed to know all the answers so Hudson asked one final question.

"But who made all the water?"

"Jesus!" came the reply.

"So you know about Jesus? That's good, I do too! So now we have to find somebody around here who doesn't, and tell them about Him."

They looked around but their family was the only one in the park.

Then one little boy asked Hudson, "Wow, how old are you?"

Jack let it slip that it was Hudson's birthday, and they were instantly invited to join the family's picnic.

"It's only hot dogs," said their mother, "but you're more than welcome to stay."

While they were eating, Jack and Hudson's stories were pulled out of them by one hundred questions. The kids were very interested in how life was in Albania and India. They asked about the work that Hudson and Jack did. The children quoted facts and figures that they had learned in their studies. They had cleared listened to missionaries at their church.

After lunch, Jack gave them a tour of the boat and outlined to them on the chart where they had been. He showed them the bay where they had endured the hurricane and the bend at Cairo. He demonstrated the little shower sprayer he had rigged up.He answered questions about the solar panels, radios and GPS unit. Then Hudson called them off the boat and handed each one of them a Klondike bar that he had purchased at the park store.

It was all too soon when the family had to leave. They exchanged e-mail addresses and promised to stay in touch. The children wanted to track their progress down to Florida. Jack and Hudson were now a family project for their homeschool.

They decided to continue a little further, even though it was getting late. They pulled into a small bay and using a bit of a leftover hot dog as bait, Hudson managed to catch four bluegill for supper.

As they sat on the back deck after supper, Hudson pulled out two cupcakes he had bought at the park store. Jack said, "Looks like God's been pretty good to you for your birthday."

"Real good, considering that a year ago I didn't know if I would live to see this day, or even if I wanted to have another birthday." Hudson paused to lick his fingers. "Yes, real good. Good food, a great party, new friends, fish and even a glorious sunset prettier than all the candles on any birthday cake anywhere."

"Amen," added Jack.

"And a prettier lake you could not find."

"Actually we're in the Tennessee River."

"It looks like a lake," said Hudson.

"But it's a river."

"What was the name of that river that leads into here, the one we were on just before the dam and the lock?"

That was a Kentucky lake," explained Jack.

"It looked like a river."

"It was a lake."

"Well Tennessee certainly has big rivers," said Hudson, trying to end the conversation.

Jack waited a minute, then leaned over and said, "Hudson, you're in Mississippi."

"Jack," said Hudson pointing his finger at him, "go to bed and stop trying to fool an old man."

But as Jack came out of the bathroom he saw Hudson going over the charts trying to figure exactly where he was.

CHAPTER SIXTEEN

In the morning when Jack checked the charts he realized they had missed their turn-off. So after pulling up the anchors and getting the engine going they headed back up the river a few hundred feet and turned into Pickwick Lake.

It wasn't long before they were going through another lock. Jack kept checking the charts, looking for a town that they could pull up at to refill their pantry. All day Wednesday they didn't see anything; Thursday they rolled past Fulton without seeing a place to pull up. On Friday it was a town called Armory they were looking for, but they didn't see much hope in that as they motored past.

"We better push to get to Columbus tomorrow. We are getting low on just about everything." Jack said Friday night.

But Columbus had no place to tie up, at least none that they could see.

Sunday dinner was peanut butter and jelly sandwiches with bread that they toasted up on the frying pan. Jack's coffee was getting weaker and weaker, trying to make the beans last until they were able to buy more. They weren't about to starve, but both were getting tired of plain soup. The crackers they had left had gone moldy and were fed to ducks and fish around their boat.

Gone were the cookies and snacks for their 4:00 p.m. tea and coffee time. Hudson tried to make the situation more tolerable by telling stories of when he had gone weeks just eating rice. This only made Jack miss rice. Their goal on Monday was to find a little town called Demopolis. On the road atlas it looked like a speck, hardly more than a few streets, but it was close to the river and they hoped to at least find a convenience store to pick up a few necessities.

When they pulled up Monday afternoon, they were surprised to be able to tie up to an actual boat dock. They found a small but complete grocery store within walking distance. They celebrated by picking up ice cream cones for the walk back to their boat. They were also surprised to find wireless Internet, so while Jack was filling their gas tanks, Hudson was checking his e-mail on Jack's computer. By the time Jack had started to fill their water tanks, Hudson was busy making supper. After a glorious meal, Hudson volunteered to do dishes to allow Jack time to check his e-mail.

"Well, I'll be Ed Harrison." said Jack slowly.

"Personally I think you make a better Jack Showen then a Ed Harrison but if you insist..." joked Hudson.

"No, I just got an e-mail from Ed Harrison, I can't quite figure out how he found me."

"I don't think I ever met anybody by that name." pondered Hudson while Jack continued to read the e-mail.

"He's an uncle. Well, Sue's uncle or great uncle or something like that." said Jack, finally making the connection. Looking up he added, "I only saw him twice, once at the wedding and once at the funeral. He was in construction. I think he's retired now. He's the only member of Sue's family that was a Christian. Anyway, he says he heard I was on a trip down to Florida by water. He says he is in a town called White City in the Panhandle. He will be there for another few weeks. He gives his phone number and says we could stop in."

Jack continued deleting most of the rest of the e-mails until he found one that made him smile. Noticing the smile getting bigger, Hudson said, "Must be from Kokila."

"How did you know?"

"I haven't seen you smile this big since the day you two met. What does she say? Anything for me?"

"Here I'll read it out loud" Jack began.
'Dear Jack and Uncle Hudson,'"

"Oh, I see you got top billing!" joked Hudson.

"Are you going to be quiet and let me read this?" said Jack, still smiling.

Then he continued, "We hope you are doing fine. It will grieve you, I'm sure, to hear that mother has had a stroke. She has just recently come home from the hospital and is doing as well as can be expected. Her speech is slow, but she can make herself understood. She talks a lot about your visit and what a good time we all had together. We are thankful that she was well when you came.

"This strain on father is visible. He tries to be strong for her sake. I have canceled my upcoming trip to India. I am also looking into having a nurse come to the house on a regular basis. Please keep us in your prayers and know that you are constantly in ours. Sincerely, Kokila."

When Jack finished reading the e-mail, Hudson got up and went to the back deck to be alone. Jack had gone to bed and was asleep by the time Hudson finally came in.

The next morning Hudson started talking. He told of meeting George and Martha for the first time, of having personality conflicts with them, differences of opinions and even outright arguments. But he talked about how their relationship had grown and all the different lessons that he and his wife had learned from them -- the struggles that they had been through together.

It took most of the day for Hudson to talk over the lifetime spent with George and Martha. But over supper he seemed to be running out of stories. He was quiet more and more. Finally, before going to bed he gave Jack this advice: "Life, is too short not to spend on the greatest adventure of all. Life is too precious to not be spent on the most valuable pursuit of all. Jack, we have got to get back to being involved in that Great Commission."

Jack noticed Hudson did not give him an option, but, acting as his father, told him that he must get back to the field. He did not know how to react to Hudson's statement. Lately he had been allowing himself to think about the possibility of going back onto some mission field someplace. Or maybe he could find a mission agency that needed an accountant in a stateside office. But there was something still missing in the equation; something the Lord had yet to clarify for him; something eluding him, almost as if it were around the bend of a river, just out of sight.

The next few days were filled with going through locks and lakes. The canals were too dirty to fish in, and when they got to the lakes they sped up to make up for lost time. Most of the time they had to wait at each lock so when they got to one where they could pull straight in, it was cause for celebration.

Jack found less and less to write in the logbook. They mostly just documented the number of miles gone and which locks they went through. He did find the books that Hudson had brought along pulling him. Most of them were about missions, some were old classics by John Wesley or Hudson Taylor, and some of them were printed just last year and talked about new trends in evangelism.

Soon it was Friday, and they were pushing to get to Mobile Bay for the weekend. Again Hudson knew of a church where they could speak. The church was not exactly in Mobile, It was sort of a suburb called Park City across the bay. The missions department had arranged for a dock at a marina starting Saturday night.

This was not a very scenic part of the trip. There were a lot of barges again and a lot of industrial docks. Suddenly there was Mobile. After being isolated on the canals and lakes and rivers for so long, the site of being right in the heart of a major city was a shock. They were glad when they could put a little bit more speed to their engine and head out across the bay away from the factories and their pollution. But it was also a little unnerving to be in such a large expanse of water.

They kept as close as they dared to the northern edge of the bay, but on their southern side they could see nothing but water. On the rivers they could navigate by sight, but here Jack had to trust his GPS unit and compass. The water was choppy and occasionally the waves were higher than what they were comfortable with. Hudson stayed seated for most of the trip, even foregoing the afternoon tea time. They found that by the time they got to the marina they were exhausted from just trying to stay balanced in the rocking boat.

They were also a little surprised that there were two men in white uniforms waiting for them, guiding them to a dock.

"You must be Mr. Rivers." they said to Hudson. "If you gentlemen would step this way we will get you signed in. We've been expecting you."

Jack and Hudson followed them to an air-conditioned office and were seated in comfortable chairs while the paperwork was brought to them.

"Would you care for some coffee, tea or a cold beverage? Mr. Spinner wanted us to have you call him as soon as you got in," said a young man as he handed Hudson a telephone. "He's on line one."
"Hudson! You caught me in between meetings, so I have to make this brief. The Block family will pick the two of you up for supper tonight. You can stay

at their house for the next few days if you don't want to stay on your boat. I've written out an itinerary for you and left it with them. Feel free to call them or me if you have any questions."

Hudson only managed an "Okay, thanks," before the line went dead.

On the way back to the boat they were given a brief tour of the marina and an explanation of the facilities available to them. They were shown the pool, the laundromat, the restrooms, the showers and the ship's store and repair facilities. They were then handed keys to the various doors that they would need and an envelope containing the password for the Internet service.

After all that Hudson did need a cup of tea and Jack felt that he could do with a cup of coffee. This was all a little too new to them. They were just finishing up their drinks when a man in his mid-50s came down the dock.

"Mr. Rivers, Mr. Showen, my name is Lee Block." he said stepping on board. "My wife and I would be delighted if you could join us for supper tonight."

After handshakes all around, they quickly washed their cups out, locked up the boat and followed Mr. Block to his car.

"We really appreciate this Mr. Block, especially since it's Jack's turn to cook tonight," said Hudson.

"Call me Lee, and it's no problem. We see it as a blessing. My wife and I are what our church calls mission liaison team members, meaning we get to host a lot of missionaries and hear their stories. Last month we had a couple from Tibet staying at our house. Amazing place. Have you ever been there?" Lee asked them.

Hudson and Jack filled him in on where they had been and served. Then they did it all over again when they got to his house and met his wife. After a delightful meal during which the conversation was mostly about missions, Lee handed Hudson a packet.

"Mark said to give this to you. It's your itinerary. He's got you speaking at a few Sunday school groups, and then at home groups Monday, Tuesday and Wednesday if you want to stay that long."

"Mark Simpson is probably the most organized missions pastor I know of," said Hudson, turning to Jack. "He could probably run any Fortune 500 company but instead he runs the missions department of Park City Wesleyan."
They looked at the schedule together and found that they were speaking separately in four different Sunday school classes in the morning, followed by

a luncheon at the church with a fifth group. Sunday night was a potluck with single adults, Monday was packed with a 7:00 a.m. men's mission breakfast, then lunch with Mark and a home group including supper in the evening. Tuesday night there was only a home group meeting in the evening, and Wednesday morning was the last appointment with a ladies brunch.

Lee then handed them the keys to the car that they had come in.

"You'll need these. There's a city map in the glove box, and Mark printed out maps to every house that you need to get to. There's also a list of phone numbers in case you get lost or need anything. The gas tank is full but there's a $50 gas card in the glove box as well, which should get you through the next few days."

"Wow." said Jack, taking the keys. "Thanks. You guys sure do a lot for your visiting missionaries."

"Well, our missionaries do a lot for us. It's exciting to be part of the global church that's involved worldwide in exciting things. We attract a lot of people with our outreaches, both locally and worldwide. That's one of the reasons why we've been able to give over a million to missions this last year."

On the drive home Jack turned to Hudson. "When did you line this all up?"

"I didn't. I just made the mistake of telling Mark that he could plug us in wherever and whenever. I forgot what a dangerous thing that is to do with a guy like Mark Simpson."

The Sunday school classes were one right after the other. Most of them were twenty to thirty people each. Hudson got the big one with about fifty. The luncheon had great food but both of them were looking around for the green bean casserole. It seemed to be missing. Sunday evening they enjoyed the casual atmosphere with the single adult group. Monday wore them out. They convinced Mark to have lunch with them on their boat. Mark was excited about Yenistan.

"I really want Park City Wesleyan to have a part in reaching this new country. I'm afraid we won't have very long. Because of the political climate in the area, we need to establish churches that could go underground if need be."

He asked Hudson a lot of questions about the different agencies that he knew of that were going in. Soon Mark had to leave for another meeting, which gave Jack and Hudson time to stretch out before the evening engagement.

Tuesday morning Hudson wanted to go shopping. So following the maps, they headed into a mall area. Walking into Wal-Mart, Hudson grabbed his own cart and said, "Meet you back here in about an hour." Then he headed out on his own.

Jack stood there for a minute, surprised at Hudson's independence. Then headed off with his own cart to pick up some socks, underwear and groceries. He found himself looking at suitcases, but really didn't know why. He checked out the sales on shirts and pants but decided he really didn't need anything new. He took advantage of the fact that he had a shopping cart and a car out in the parking lot to stock up on canned goods and bags of rice and noodles. He picked up some fresh fruit and checked out the mangoes but he didn't think that they would pass Hudson's inspection. He then went to the international food section and picked up some Indian spices and jars of pickle and chutney.

By the time he moved out of the checkout lane he had no idea if the hour was up or not. But he saw Hudson seated next to his cart waiting for him. It looked like Hudson had done as much shopping as he had.

"What's in all those bags?" he asked Hudson.
"My new laptop," Hudson replied as he got up and headed out towards the car.

Stunned, Jack followed him.

After lunch on the boat Hudson got out the boxes and bags that he had just brought home.

"You should have seen the look on the face of that geeky teenager behind the counter! I surprised him by knowing all about RAM and memory and performance and all the technical jargon. What? Do I need to be stuck back in the horse and buggy days just because I'm older?"

It occurred to Jack that he had viewed Hudson as being behind the times and technology, probably just because he was older. But here was Hudson not only loading up his laptop with all the latest programs but downloading Google and Skype. Before long he had Pandora up and running with Gospel hymns. He even talked Jack into setting up a Skype account. Leaving him to his work, Jack grabbed the laundry and headed down the dock. After getting the machines filled and running, he strolled round the marina and saw a series of boats all on their sides behind the building.

"What happened here?" He asked one of the attendants.

"Well, that hurricane that passed through here a while ago, knocked over that big yacht there," he said pointing to the first one. "Then one after another just like dominoes, they all went over. The last one we found in the pool. It had the least amount of damage. We've got to let these sit here until the insurance company can come take a look at them."

It was such a different world than the one Jack was used to. When he got back to the boat with clean dry clothes, Hudson was on a Skype video call to George and Martha, filling them in on the details of their trip and asking about Martha's health.

Walking out to the car to go to the evening appointment, Jack turned to him and said, "You continue to surprise me Hudson."

"Good," he said, "and I'm not done yet. I've got a few more surprises up my sleeve."

Jack did not know whether to be impressed or scared.

CHAPTER SEVENTEEN

At the Wednesday morning ladies brunch, Hudson was a big hit. It was clear that a few of the ladies considered him an eligible bachelor.

On the way back to their boat they stopped at Lee's to drop off the car. Lee's wife brought them to the marina and sent them off with a gift basket of homemade baked goods. It was tempting to stay longer at the marina. They had not even been in the pool. However both of them felt the urge to get back on the water, not so much to get away from Park City; nor was it a feeling of missing the traveling. It was more a sense that they needed to get to the "next thing" even though they were not sure what that next thing was.

By late afternoon they were back on the water trying to cross the bay to find a good anchorage for the night. Their next goal was to see Sue's Uncle Ed in White City. They hoped to be there Saturday night. As the sun was just setting, they cut through the canal that led from Bon Secour Bay to Oyster Bay and dropped anchor for the night.

The sun was barely up when Jack started the engines in the morning and got the boat going. Hudson definitely was *not* up. It was at least another good hour before he dragged himself out of bed. It took him longer that morning to go through his usual morning routine.

"My throat feels horrible," said Hudson with a graveled voice.

After not much breakfast, Hudson gargled with salt water, took some ibuprofen and went back to bed.

Their surroundings were a little different now. They were in saltwater. There was more of a tropical feel to the breeze. Jack did not find it difficult to follow the canals and cut across the open bays even without Hudson's help. Hudson did manage to get up now and then but only to get something to drink and grab some more ibuprofen.

By noon Jack was pulling into Pensacola Bay. He was hoping to find a place to tie up or anchor so that he could fix lunch but halfway across the bay he forgot about lunch. The engine suddenly stopped.

"Why are you stopping?" asked Hudson from his bed.

"Trust me, I have no idea," replied a panic stricken Jack, running to the back of the boat to check on the engine.

They drifted for a few minutes while Jack took the engine cover off and tried to diagnose the problem.

It all looked normal, maybe a little warm, but that would not be too unusual since the temperature outside was a little warmer too.

He went back to the helm and tried to restart the engine. It turned over but didn't catch. He knew from his experience he could probably fix the engine, but not out here in the middle of Pensacola Bay. For a while Hudson and Jack just looked at each other not quite sure what to do next.

"Well, shall I call you a tow truck?" asked Hudson finally.

"Sure."

"Okay, you're a tow truck," laughed Hudson.

"Seriously, what are we going to do? We can't just drift here, waiting for the next boat to pass." said Jack, a little frustrated.

"Well first we're going to pray, and then you're going to turn on that radio there and call for help." And then Hudson began to pray. At the end of the prayer Jack flipped on the radio and dialed cChannel Sixteen.

"Umm, if anybody is listening, we are out in the middle of Pensacola Bay and our engine just stopped, not sure what to do now," said a very uncertain Jack.

"Well Captain, this is the Coast Guard. Give me a description of your boat, with it's name. If you know your GPS coordinates you can add those too." said a very professional voice.

"We are a Seagoing Houseboat, with the name "Ekbalo" and I can probably get you the coordinates in a minute or two."

"Hey Ekbalo, I think I see you. Honk your horn." said a much different voice.

After Jack gave a few toots the voice came back. "I'm coming right behind you. Captain Toad to Coast Guard: I'll give them a hand and let you know if we need anything else. Captain Toad out."

"Okay Toad, we will be listening, Coast Guard out."

Within minutes their boat was approached by a tugboat that looked like it came from Toys R Us. It was about eight feet long and painted bright colors. Its bumpers were covered with rope and its captain's face, when it appeared, was covered with hair. He had a strong resemblance to Santa Claus. As he came up alongside, he cut his engine, and tossed them a rope.

When the two boats were tied securely together,

the man introduced himself as Albert Towe, a retired commander in the Navy.

"Toad was a childhood nickname that stuck with me." he explained.

"Retired Petty Officer Rivers at your service." said Hudson with a salute.

"I've given up saluting since I retired." said Toad, and held out his hand.

Hudson shook it and said, "I see you've been promoted to captain though."

"Yeah, something my wife did at my retirement party, but what seems to be the problem with your boat?"

Jack took him over to the engine compartment and they both looked at it for a while, getting out a flashlight to look in the corners and crevices. They got quite dirty in the process.

"Aha," said Jack, half in and half out of the engine compartment. "The wire from the distributor cap shorted out. I guess it was the wrong size and shorted out on the engine. I should have caught that when I was first working on the engine."

"Well, I don't live too far from here. I can tow you to

my dock and see if I have an extra cable in the tool shed. If not, there's an auto parts store not too far down the road," said Toad, wiping his hands on a rag.

Hudson went with him over to his boat and Jack stayed on theirs for the short trip. This gave Jack his first opportunity to really look at Captain Toad's boat. It was a scaled-down version of a full size tug boat. It looked homemade, but it was the most shipshape craft he had seen on the trip so far.

About a half hour later he was tying up to a dock. Jack was shown the tool shed and was given free reign. Meanwhile, Captain Toad took Hudson into the house talking all the time about their days in the Navy.

Just before they went into the house Jack overheard Hudson asking, "Did you hear about the guy that could actually walk on water?"

Within half an hour Jack had found a suitable cable and replaced it and had the engine running again. He cleaned his hands with hand cleanser in the shed and made his way to the house. He was ordered to pull up to the table by the captain's wife and a bowl of chicken soup was placed before him.

"Best thing for a cold like Hudson's," said the charming Mrs. Towe. She refilled Hudson's bowl for the second time. Just looking at Hudson, Jack could tell he was feeling better.

As they got up to leave, Toad shook Hudson's hand and said, "Thanks for the encouraging words, Hudson, I'll be sure to keep Jesus in the boat."

 A few minutes later Jack and Hudson headed back to their houseboat with a jar of home canned chicken soup and a small bottle of raw apple cider vinegar. "Best thing for a cold and sore throat, they told me." said Hudson.

On their way again Jack increased the engines speed just a little to make up for lost time. Feeling better, Hudson took over his position on the couch reading the charts and checking the maps.

"You never told me you were in the Navy," Jack said as they pulled through Fort Walton Beach.

"You never asked," joked Hudson. "There's not enough time before I die to tell you everything that I've seen and done."

They found a place to anchor for the night and by putting in a long day on Friday they made it past Panama City by the evening. Other than talking about the next landmark or what city they were passing through, conversation was at a minimum.

Jack was thinking about the future. Here they were in Florida already. In a few days, maybe a week, they would be at the journey's end. Then what? And what about Hudson? To Jack it seemed that Hudson was thinking about the same things. Hudson had become a great friend ... more like family. Jack could not see himself dropping Hudson off someplace and saying goodbye. But how could Jack take care of Hudson? Could he get a job, buy a condo and care for Hudson in his old age? As much as Jack liked Hudson, that thought scared him. And what if he went back to the field? What would Hudson do? But if Hudson had any other plans, he sure wasn't sharing them. Jack even looked through the logbook entries to see if Hudson was writing anything down.

It was almost a relief then, on Saturday, to pull through White City, and tie up to a dock and call Uncle Ed. At least Ed would provide conversation and get his mind off the future. Within a few minutes Sue's Uncle Ed pulled up in an old Suburban.

"Hop in you two. I've got a few things left to do today at the job site. You can come along and give me a hand." said Ed from behind the steering wheel.

The short drive gave them just enough time for Jack to introduce Hudson and to fill Ed in a bit about the trip. When they got to the work site it was obvious Ed intended to get a few hours of labor out of both of them. Hudson was sent to sweep up after some carpenters and Jack was to mix mortar while Ed laid up the few remaining blocks in a wall.

Judging by the number of children running around that he was working on an orphanage.

"I thought you retired," said Jack, delivering another bucket full of mortar.

"I did. This sure beats golfing," said Ed with a laugh. "These kids need some more room. And I need a place to park the trailer now and then. Seems like a good trade-off to me."

Jack knew that there was more to it than that. Ed was always giving of his time and energy.

While they worked, Jack filled Ed in on most of the rest of the trip. He left out the bits about not being sure of the future. He didn't want to talk about that now.

By 5:00 p.m. they had wrapped up, cleaned up and closed up for the day. On the way to Ed's trailer they stopped at Subway and picked up sandwiches for the evening meal. Ed's home for the time being was a twenty-four foot trailer parked under a shed roof. The trailer only took up half the room under the roof which gave Ed a sizable porch. Here they pulled up plastic chairs to a plastic table and ate their sandwiches.

They talked about missions, they talked about Sue, and they talked about the kids in the orphanage. They talked about India and Albania. And around a small campfire they talked late into the night.

The next morning they went to the church that many of the children went to. It was small and white and had the typical steeple and bell tower. There could hardly have been fifty people, including all the children and Uncle Ed greeted them all. He seemed to know everybody's name and if people did not call him "uncle" Ed, it was either "grandpa" or "brother".

It was a far cry from Park City Wesleyan. There was no worship band or orchestra, no air conditioning or padded pews. They sang three hymns from the hymnal and fanned themselves with their bulletins. The pastor had no fancy overheads or sermon illustrations. He spoke straight from the Bible. When they left, Jack and Hudson felt just as spiritually full as they had at any of the churches they'd been to on this trip.

They sat under the porch in the afternoon. Hudson had found a lounge chair and was taking a snooze. Jack and Uncle Ed were drinking iced tea and lemonade and munching on some pretzels. They were chatting pleasantly about family, the sermon, and even the weather, when Ed dropped the bomb.

"So what about your future?"

Jack was quiet at first, and then said, "I haven't thought much about it, well … that's really a lie. I've thought a lot about it, it's just that I don't know what to think about it. I really can't think of anything I want to do. I was hoping this trip would help sort things out. If anything I'm more confused now."

"Hudson has become a good friend and I want to make sure he's taken care of. Maybe we can keep the boat here and I can help you at the orphanage. I just don't know."

"Well let's start with what you do know. You can't stay here and help me at the orphanage. I'm here just a few months out of the year and you are the worst mortar mixer I've had in a long time," laughed uncle Ed. "Second, you do not have to take care of Hudson. Why he's probably a year or two younger than I am. He can take care of himself and most important of all, he wants to take care of himself. He doesn't want or need you, in fact you probably need him more!"

"Amen" said a sleepy Hudson with one eye open.

"And I think you do know what your future is going to hold, but you have not grabbed onto it yet."

"So are you going to tell me?" asked Jack.

"Missions."

"I always figured I would go back to the field one day, but I don't know if I'm ready yet," answered Jack.

"You may never think you are ready. Your readiness is not as important as God's timing."

"You think the timing is right?" Jack asked with a little hesitation. He was not used to such straight talk. He was almost afraid of what Ed would say next but everything he had said so far rang true in his heart.

"Why, this whole trip is God's way of launching you out. That's kind of obvious to me." Ed was quiet for a while, letting this sink in.

"Okay, then where?"

"Well, if you ask me, this place Hudson's been talking about, this, Yahoostan, sounds like a good fit."

Jack laughed. "Yenistan. However I think I like your version better. Do you think I can do it? I mean, alone, without Sue. She was such a big part of the ministry."

189

"You would not be alone, you'd be part of the team that's over there and you would have a team back here. And it's not up to me to decide if you can do it or not, that's up to God. Your role is to either agree with him or disagree with him."

After a pause, Ed continued, "When you are on the Mississippi, what was your speed? How fast were you going through St. Louis?"

"Well, about 10 or 15 miles an hour," guessed Jack.

"Was your engine turning that fast?"

"No it was barely turning over. It was mostly the river pushing us."

"And if you turned your boat around and started to head upstream with your engine still turning at the same speed, what would've happened?"

"We would still be heading downstream. We would have had to really fight to go up river." Jack was starting to see where this was going.

"You do not have to do it all on your own power. You have a river pushing you; helping you. Jack. You and Sue got into God's river of missions and he is still pushing you on. Sure there's been a few lakes and eddies along the way, but when you look at it He's still in control and it looks pretty clear as to what your next steps are." Ed let that sink in while he went into the trailer and brought out hamburgers for the grill.

After he got the fire going, and the burgers on, he turned to Jack. "Just remember, God's river has been building up steady since day one. Now that it's getting close to the end, it's built up quite a momentum. I would hate to be in a little boat trying to fight that current. Now, get into the trailer and bring out the buns. These burgers won't take long."

By the time he had come back out, Hudson was up and rubbing his eyes.

"Nicest place to take a nap that I've found in a long time, especially when you wake up to the smell of hamburgers." said Hudson, sampling the iced tea.

"Well you're welcome any time I'm here. You'd be welcome wherever I am. Keep in touch. Sometimes I find myself farther down in Florida. Might maybe be 'round your neck of the woods."

Jack was glad that during supper no one brought up the topic of his future. The conversation was lighter and easier. He felt almost tired from all the heavy thinking that afternoon.

The next day, Ed stopped by their boat halfway through the morning to see them off.

"You keep in touch," he said to Jack. "I want to know what happens at the end of this trip."

"You stay in touch too," he said to Hudson, "and keep an eye on that boy. Don't let him get into any trouble." Then he walked back to his Suburban and went back to work.

CHAPTER EIGHTEEN

They had made it through Lake Wimico before Hudson thought about making lunch.

"You want cheese on your sandwich?" Was the most Hudson had said to Jack since they left White City.

Jack wanted to talk but didn't know what to say. Hudson was clearly not bringing up any topics for discussion. He had spent longer in his Bible reading and prayer time, even singing three hymns instead of just one today, almost as if trying to avoid conversation. Jack was left to have conversations with himself as he steered the boat towards Apalachicola.

Their plan was to stop there and get a feel for how they should make the jump to Tampa Bay. About three in the afternoon they tied up to a dock. Hudson still was not saying much more than what was needed to secure the boat and get ready for a little shopping trip.

It was easy to find a grocery store and it was easier still to find people that would give them advice on how to cross the Bay. It seemed as though everyone had their own opinion.

"Leave at dusk," said one. "Leave at dawn." said

another. One sailor suggested that they wait till the rain storm came in and leave just as it was letting up.

"The Northwest wind will blow you right to Tampa in one good day," he said. But then when he found out that they were in a houseboat and not a sailboat, he was quick to change his advice. "Stay here, you'll never make it," he said.

The consensus was that they should hug the coast as far east as possible then take a good clear day to make a straight run for Cedar Key. From there pick another good clear day for a straight run to Tarpon Springs where they could tuck into the intracoastal waterway again. So with full tanks of gas and water and enough food for a few days in the kitchen, they headed out through Apalachicola Bay.

It was after breakfast the next day that the silence was finally broken. First it happened in Jack's mind. It was like a switch was turned on or a cloud was lifted. He finally knew what he felt called to do. He just did not know how it would affect Hudson and the other people now in his life.

The dishes were done, and Hudson had come up to the couch with a cup of tea, settling himself down to go over the charts.

"Hudson, I'm going back on the field." was all he could say at first.

"Okay… where and when?" was all Hudson replied.

"Well, I'm thinking Yenistan, if your friends will have me. And as far as when, I think I'll have to raise some support, so I'm not sure. There are a lot of details that need to be sorted out before I go."

"What made you choose to go?" asked Hudson.

"Well a lot of things," Jack replied. "Some of the things that you've been saying have been sticking in my mind. What my Uncle Ed said, well, let's just say he put a different point of view to it. But it wasn't until yesterday and today that I think I actually heard God tell me it was time."

"You '*think*' you heard God?"

"No, I'm sure, and it's not as though he hadn't been talking. It's that I shut up long enough and was quiet enough to hear him speaking."

Hudson was quiet, then setting his tea cup down, he folded his hands in prayer and said, "Thank you Jesus!"

Surprised, Jack asked, "You are in favor of this?"

"In favor? It's what I've been praying for since we started this trip!"

"What?"

Hudson cleared his throat and settled back on the couch. "One of the reasons I wanted to come on this trip was to get you back on the field. I will admit that at first I was only thinking about getting me out of the nursing home. But it became clearer as we went along that God had a plan to use this trip, not only to get you to the place where you are now, but to get me involved in helping you."

Hudson paused and looked out the window. "This river trip has pulled me out of a slump and brought me to a place where at first I did not want to go, yet how do you argue with the force of the river? Now I see clearly that God is not done with me, but can use me to help you in your ministry."

"You make it sound like I have some sort of great and glorious ministry. Don't forget I'm an accountant. I'm not going to plant churches or save a bunch of souls ... at most I can save some dollars and cents."

Hudson pointed his finger straight at Jack and with a stern fatherly look in his eyes said, "Don't ever underestimate the gift that God has given you or the tools he has given you to minister with. All gifts and talents are equal in his eyes." He then softened his look, "Now, we've got some work to do and just a few more days until we get to Matlacha." Hudson got up and went back to a duffel bag where he pulled an envelope out of a book. "Here, I'll steer, you read." he said as he handed Jack the letter.

The letter was from Bill, the janitor, not the pastor.

"Dear Hudson," it read, "Now that you are on your way, I can let you in on a little secret. I feel that Jack still has a lot to give in terms of service on the field. I hope this trip will convince him of that fact. Should he come to the point where he is ready to head out on the field, let him know I will support him in the amount of $500 a month. This is due to the fact that one of my missionaries that I have been supporting has retired as of August 1. I am putting this amount in a bank account until Jack needs it. My prayers are with the two of you as he is going to need you to be on his support team when he goes."

"$500 a month? I figure that's about all he makes. How can he afford that?" Jack was almost yelling.

"I asked him that on the phone shortly after I got the letter. It was one of the main reasons I got the phone. Seems like from a young age he's been saving his money. He started out by buying a small house that had been foreclosed, then renting it out. He now owns about five houses, free and clear.

With the income he supports four or five missionaries. Amazing man, that Bill," said Hudson as he handed the wheel back to Jack.

Doing a bit of mental math, Jack figured it would not take much more support, added to his own income, before he would feel comfortable in going overseas.

"You could revisit some of the churches we were at. It won't take much more before you're fully supported and can leave. Being single, you would not need a large budget."

Hudson must've been reading his mind, Jack thought.

They anchored early. They had reached the end of the bay and the point from which they would start their crossing to Cedar Key.

This was Apalachee Bay. They dropped their anchor behind a small sandbar. It was only about fifteen feet wide and maybe now hundred and fifty feet long. It probably appeared due to the hurricane and probably would disappear in the next storm, but for right now it was their own private island. They did some swimming and general laying about. Jack got out his camera and took a few pictures of Hudson in a deck chair on his own private island. Jack spent that evening listening to weather reports. Hudson spent it writing in the ship's log.

Tuesday, October 23.
Finally at long last, Jack has made a commitment to go back on the field. That to me is more exciting than finding this private island that we are now anchored to. To think that a few months ago I was sitting in a nursing home in Chicago, and today I'm sitting in a deck chair on my own island is a testimony to the goodness of God. But more than that, God's goodness is seen in that he has called both of us back into service for his kingdom. We are only waiting for favorable weather to cross the bay to Cedar Key. It will be a big jump and for the first time in the trip we will not be in sight of land. We have plenty of gas and food and could stay out for a couple of days actually. And there are probably plenty of shrimp boats that could give us a hand if we need it. Jack is listening to the weather reports and says that we should try it early in the morning. He is afraid that Thursday would be too rainy. I think that now that he has made the decision to go he is in a hurry to get to Matlacha. Jack took a picture of me sitting on my island, as soon as I can I will post it on my Facebook page. I hope all the folks at Baptist Manor see it. Maybe I will send them a print.

With the favorable forecast they set out as soon as it was light enough. Hudson ate his breakfast alone while Jack was steering. Then Hudson took over and Jack sat down at the table. Next to his plate was an envelope.

"What's this?" he asked Hudson.

"Open it."

Inside was a check made out to Jack for the price that he had paid Hudson for the boat.

"Again I have to ask, what's this?"

"I decided not to sell the boat after all. I don't think you're going to need it after we get to Florida and I've come to like living on board. Besides, you're going to have some expenses when you land in Florida."

"Oh, and don't I have anything to say about it?"

"Okay, do you want to hold on to this boat and pay all the maintenance on it while you're in some far-off country or would you rather have the cash?"

Jack thought for a minute. "Cash." he said as he put the check in his wallet.

As Jack started to eat his breakfast, Hudson kept talking. "Next item: support raising. You are going to need a team leader stateside that can coordinate prayer support and financial support. For that position I nominate a certain Hudson Rivers. Now, you don't have to pick me, but I know you and I'm committed to your call. After these past few months you seem like family to me."

Jack swallowed his eggs. "I was hoping you would volunteer. I can't think of anyone I would rather have. I'm just not sure of your job description."

"Well we have a few days to work that out. And look, the way I work it may seem like I'm trying to charge ahead faster than you may want to go. At any point feel free to stop me. You are the boss, you have full veto rights. It's just that I have a lot more years of experience and sometimes I get it into my head that I know it all. I know I don't, but sometimes I may act that way. And by the way I have some more confessions to make," said Hudson, almost apologetically.

Jack tried to look surprised. "No... really? What now?"

"I have been keeping in touch with the churches we have been at and have dropped hints that you might be coming back to raise support. All we have to do now is write them a formal letter, or e-mail, and get you scheduled. We may have to get you a car."

Jack could see that Hudson was deep in thought over all the details. It took Jack a little time to get used to Hudson in control, but he was good at it. Jack remembered the first shopping trip to stock the boat and that Hudson was the one that remembered toilet paper. As Jack's mind was filled with other mountains that must be moved, he let Hudson handle the details.

For the rest of that day as they took turns steering, they went over details and plans. What groups they would set up for prayer support, how they would handle finances and what plans they would need to put in place in case of emergencies.

"Wait, we don't even know if the group in Yenistan want me to come yet," said Jack putting the brakes on their planning.

"Yes we do. That's another thing I have to ask for your forgiveness for. I've already told him about you and that you would probably come. I filled out your application and you have been accepted, you just need to sign on the line."

Jack just looked at Hudson. On the one hand he was annoyed at his meddling. He felt that Hudson had overstepped the boundary of their friendship. In the next instant he realized it wasn't Hudson, it was the Holy Spirit getting everything ready beforehand.

"Okay, thanks," said Jack, and they went back to making plans.

Because they were in open water and were

following a compass reading, many times they just clamped the steering wheel in one place and went about their business, occasionally looking up to check for ships or other boats. They both sat down to lunch at the dining room table while the boat obediently followed the compass.

Jack got out his computer and composed letters and lists. Hudson got out his and wrote e-mails that he would send out as soon as they got connected.

"I think I need a home church, some body of believers that I can relate to," said Jack.

"Well, I think it would do you good to meet with the pastor in Matlacha. We are old friends and there are a lot of other good souls in the church. Let's see what happens when you get there, you might feel at home," replied Hudson.

It surprised them when they looked up and saw Cedar Key. They were going to make it just before sunset. Jack picked up the radio and tried to call a marina. He reached another boater who gave him the option of the public dock or a private marina. Jack chose the marina because it had a better chance of having an Internet connection and he'd been a few days without a good hot shower. A washing machine would be a welcome item too.

Early in the morning he was glad of this choice. The

rains came. It was evident from the weather that they would have to wait out the day tied up to the dock. It was not an unwelcome interruption. They had a lot of work they wanted to get done. Besides the dirty clothes, some basic repairs to the boat and a quick trip to a store for some fresh fruit and supplies would be in order. They made a lot of progress in terms of preparation for Jack's move to Yenistan. They hardly noticed that the rain had let up in the early evening when the sky turned a bright blue just before sunset.

They were ready at the crack of dawn on Friday to make the jump to Tarpon Springs. This jump would not be as scary as the last one because they were veterans at it now, or so they felt. They would also be within sight of land most of the way.

They were able to get a little bit more work done on the trip, but Jack stayed behind the wheel most of the time, steering the boat through the shallows that were surprisingly far out into the bay. Time passed quickly and before they knew it they were anchoring in a protective little bay near Tarpon Springs. The next day they would arrive in Matlacha.

"This is it, the trip is over," thought Jack, as he did the dishes that evening. Hudson was talking on the phone to his friend in Matlacha. He was checking the charts and making pencil notes on them. He was asking about a car. He was asking about the health of a variety of friends. He was asking about the church. And Jack was asking himself, what is going on.

Again he felt caught up in the river. It seemed as though he was being swept along. He felt as if he was just a small part of this whole "getting to Yenistan" thing. Then he realized he was. This was more than just him traveling to a country to do bookkeeping. This was about churches reaching the lost, about nations, about God's plan for expanding the kingdom. He was slowly coming out of his isolation and realizing he was a part of a team now. He suddenly had a mental picture: it was no longer Hudson and himself on a small houseboat on a river. The boat had grown to the size of the Dixie Queen. Hundreds of people were on board, being pulled down the river with the same goal, with the same destination, with the same purpose.

That night he dreamt he was in a strange country speaking Russian.

CHAPTER NINETEEN

Jack stood next to the dark blue minivan. His bags were inside, a thermos filled with hot coffee was next to the driver's seat, a bag of snacks within reach and on the front passenger seat were maps, a calendar and his itinerary.

Four weeks ago they had pulled in to Matlacha and tied up to the dock where the houseboat still sat. Four weeks ago he met the pastor of the church where Hudson was now on staff as a missions pastor emeritus. Three weeks ago Jack had moved into an apartment above the garage of a member of the church. That week he also set up two bank accounts that he could draw money from when in Yenistan. They also had seen a lawyer and drawn up papers for power of attorney.

Then, borrowing a car, Jack had driven over to his parents condo and spent a week catching them up on the last few months. There were many things that they could not understand about his decision to go back overseas. They had found jobs in their area for him and thought that he could settle down on the East Coast of Florida. On his trip back to Matlacha, Jack thanked God for a man in his life like Hudson and others like Uncle Ed and Bill.

After supper one night, Hudson brought up the subject. "It's not a subject people like to talk about, but maybe after breakfast tomorrow we had better draw up a will for you." All that night Jack had thought about it.

After breakfast Hudson got out his laptop. "I've got a program here with all the legal jargon. All you have to do is fill in the blanks." He said. Some questions were hard, like legal residence. Other than a P.O. Box up near Chicago, Jack had no legal residence. "We will fill that in later," said Hudson, moving on to the next questions. Next of kin: no brothers, no sisters and no children. What was he going to do? "Why don't you stick it all in a trust fund and decide the outcome later. You can pick a charity or church or something," was Hudson's advice.

"What do you want done with your remains?" This question was harder because it brought up a lot of painful memories of Sue. But Jack was ready. He had thought a lot about it in the last few days.

"Bury me where I fall. I don't want my remains to be shipped around, too much hassle; too much money. I figure God can find me when it's time for the resurrection, wherever I am. I don't want somebody to have to go through what I went through with Sue."

"You never did tell me about the memorial service," said Hudson. "You told me it was memorable, but you never told me why."

Jack was quiet for a while, retrieving memories.

"You have to understand, we had a nice service in Albania with friends that knew us and shared my sorrow. When it came to the American service, I was tired and wanted it to be over, so I said a few things that I probably shouldn't have said."

"Oh, like what?" Hudson leaned forward and pushed the computer off to one side.

"Well you see, I got tired of people trying to console me by telling me that Sue was now an angel; or that it was God's best will; or that Sue was saved from some future calamity that would be worse; or for saying things like Sue will always be around me. So when I got up behind the pulpit I told them they had their theology wrong. I told them they had to read their Bible more and get the truth. Sue was not an angel, angels were serving Sue. Sue was not ever with me, Sue was forever with Jesus and I thought that once you started hanging around Jesus you wouldn't want to hang around anybody else for all eternity. And as for the statement that God saved Sue from a future calamity by taking her home early, I told them that's like the doctor cutting off your hand so that you wouldn't get a splinter in your finger. I told them the truth was more like, God gave Sue early retirement with full benefits." Jack was quiet for a minute. "I guess there were a few other things. I think it really shocked them, but I told them that lies and stories cannot comfort those who mourn. But the Bible says to weep with those who weep, and what I needed was people to share my sorrow and not try to put a different spin on it."

It was Hudson's turn to be quiet, but a smile spread across his face. "Bravo," was all he said, and he got up to make lunch.

After lunch Hudson wrote up a quick document about what hymns Jack wanted sung and what Scriptures Jack wanted recited at his own service.

It was surprising how things were coming together, but Hudson had a way of blending the right people into teams that got things done. And Hudson knew people. LOTS of people, people from all walks of life. Upper-class, lower-class, it didn't matter. It seemed like Hudson could relate to anyone.

This trip was mapped out to take him on a zigzag tour back up the course of the river. He would be meeting with every church that they had stopped at on their way down as well as individuals that Hudson introduced him to through e-mail and over the phone. Jack had gotten his own address book out and had contacted people he had not thought of for months now, but all were glad to know that he was heading back overseas and would love to see him and talk about supporting him through prayers and giving. The family they had met on Hudson's birthday was organizing an international dinner to raise money for his trip.

Halfway up the continental United States Jack was glad he would be able to spend a few days with George, Martha and Kokila. They had been particularly excited when Hudson called them with the news.

The trip would end when he reached Hudson's storage unit. Jack had a list of things that Hudson wanted him to bring down to Florida and the rest was to be given away or sold. While there, he would meet with Bill and was even offered a chance to preach at Bill's little Baptist church.

The boat was back in Hudson's name. It was secured to the side of the little general store with sturdier ropes. It had a new heavy gauge electrical cord hooking it on a more permanent basis to shore power. Hudson had started in on a few remodeling projects, making it more user-friendly for him and also less of a boat and more of a home.

There had been several meetings with the pastor of the church in Matlacha and after several interviews with the board of the church, Jack was accepted as a missionary. This meant that the funds that he raised could go through their books and Hudson could then deposit the money into Jack's bank account. With the help of the accounting department at the church they set up a budget, putting aside money for taxes and emergencies. They found no health insurance that would cover Jack while he was overseas that was affordable, so the emergency fund would be used if he needed anything major done health wise.

The van came along at the last minute. Originally he was looking for a small compact car that would get good gas mileage, but an older lady in the church was selling her van at a very good price. With the van he would not have to stop at hotels along the way, he could just roll out a sleeping bag on a camping mattress in the back. Most of the nights however he would be staying at people's houses along the way.

It had taken them about two months to get down to Florida and now it would take him about two months to get back to Chicago, driving back and forth across the river. He never thought of it as going back home, or even retracing his steps. This was not a return trip in his mind but a continuation of the one he'd been on not just for the last two months but for years.

He felt comfortable leaving Hudson in the company of his friends in Florida. They would take good care of him. That was a good thing because Jack

211

needed Hudson now more than ever. Hudson was his link to his supporters and prayer partners. Jack felt that he had a very solid foundation from which to minister. He felt, even now, prayers being offered up on his behalf.

They were not there this morning. There had been a farewell party last night at the church. Today it was only Hudson standing at the end of the dock, on his own, no cane in sight. Hudson, who was in a wheelchair when he first met him, was now standing on his own without any aid. That was good; that was the image Jack wanted to keep in his mind because Jack was going to lean on Hudson for the next several years.

He needed to get going. But there was a part of him that didn't want to go. Hudson prayed for him, for safety on the road. They hugged. Then Jack got behind the driver's seat and set out on his journey. When he checked his rearview mirror, he caught a sight of Hudson talking to the man who was fishing off the dock. "Probably he's talking to him about a fisherman named Peter." thought Jack.

He didn't want quiet. He flipped on the radio and hit the first station that he came to. It was a country-western station but the song that had just started seem to fit his mood. It was not a particularly religious song that he sang out loud as he headed towards the highway.

"I'm saying goodbye to Memphis,
Where my dreams
were supposed to come true,
I'm saying goodbye to the good-time lies,
And the pain they put you through.
I'm saying goodbye to Memphis,
Where my dreams
were supposed to come true,
I'm saying goodbye to Memphis,
But I'm saying hello to you."

Ship's log, November... Monday.
It's been a while since I've written in the log and it will be a while or perhaps never that I will write again. This boat may never sail again. Ekbalo has made her last voyage but in a sense the trip goes on. It was the voyage I had dreamed of with my wife, then thought that I lost when I lost her. It was Jack that made the dream possible again but it was also the boat that made Jack's dream a reality too. Life is like that. God is like that.

The boat is back in my name, but it is a different boat, I may have to change the name. Now it's become my home, perhaps my last.

Jack left today. He left a much different man than when he started out, but then again so am I. Both of us had deep holes in our lives and for a while we helped each other heal. I think we were more

213

similar when the trip started, now we have found healing but it has made us different from each other. I need to stay, Jack needs to move on.

I will take this month to make some changes on the boat. I need a refrigerator. I need a permanent desk. I'll get some more lights in this place. I may get a small TV. I am definitely going to get an air conditioner but I can wait on that for a while.

I like it here. There is a trailer park just up the road, and I have made some friends there. At the church there are always activities. So many in fact that if I did them all I would not have time for fishing. I intend on fishing, in fact I caught dinner three times last week.

This is nothing like retirement. I feel that even though I am not going to Yenistan, I am there in spirit and in mind. All I can say is, "Hallelujah!" God is not finished with me yet!

AUTHOR BIO

Dan Smeenge has lives on five continents and several islands. His most interesting house guests have been Kechua Indians, Kosovan refugees, one thousand loose baby chicks, and tarantulas. He is father and grandfather to a wonderfully crazy, totally non-related, multicolored family. He's moved over fifty times, once being a journey down the Mississippi. His first book, "Redeeming River" is also available on Master Releases.

Cover image: Thank you Johnny Kilroy of unsplash.com